He unbuttoned his shirt and Olivia swallowed, trying to keep her stare on the bullet wound rather than the broad expanse of bare chest.

Damn. She was in some kind of trouble.

She fumbled with the bottle of water, grasping it as he reached for her chin and pulled her face up, making eye contact.

"If this is a problem for you Olivia, I can get someone else to clean the wound."

"It would help if you didn't…touch me while I'm trying to work."

A sultry smile bowed his lips and before she realized what was happening, he bent down and took complete possession of her mouth, gently, slowly exploring, stoking the fire burning in her veins. Then he let her go, grasping her upper arms to keep her from falling.

"You said you hadn't been kissed enough after your near-death experience. I thought I'd take the opportunity to rectify that."

JAN HAMBRIGHT

The
PHANTOM of
BLACK'S COVE

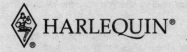

HARLEQUIN®

TORONTO • NEW YORK • LONDON
AMSTERDAM • PARIS • SYDNEY • HAMBURG
STOCKHOLM • ATHENS • TOKYO • MILAN • MADRID
PRAGUE • WARSAW • BUDAPEST • AUCKLAND

Recycling programs
for this product may
not exist in your area.

ISBN-13: 978-0-373-69408-2

THE PHANTOM OF BLACK'S COVE

ABOUT THE AUTHOR

Jan Hambright penned her first novel at seventeen, but claims it was pure rubbish. However, it did open the door on her love for storytelling. Born in Idaho, she resides there with her husband, three of their five children, a three-legged watch dog and a spoiled horse named Texas, who always has time to listen to her next story idea while they gallop along.

A self-described adrenaline junkie, Jan spent ten years as a volunteer EMT in rural Idaho, and jumped out of an airplane at ten-thousand feet attached to a man with a parachute, just to celebrate turning forty. Now she hopes to make your adrenaline level rise along with that of her danger-seeking characters. She would like to hear from her readers and hopes you enjoy the story world she has created for you. Jan can be reached at P.O. Box 2537, McCall, Idaho 83638.

Books by Jan Hambright

CAST OF CHARACTERS

Jack Trayborne—Untouchable and mysterious, Jack uses his extraordinary abilities to protect the citizens of Black's Cove. But can he allow a nosy blonde journalist in on his secret without risking everything, including his heart?

Olivia Morgan—She's a tenacious freelance journalist looking for the truth behind a mysterious medical treatment called NPQ. But someone wants to prevent her from ever getting the story out.

Dr. Martin Trayborne—The patriarch of the Trayborne family died ten years earlier, but he left the key to Pandora's box in the hands of his grandson, Jack, before he died. Does someone want to open it now?

Rick Dowdy—He was a test subject in Dr. Trayborne's experiments, and he shares some of the same paranormal abilities as Jack. But does he use them for good...or evil?

Diana Moore—Another former test subject, the dangerous beauty would like nothing more than to get close to Jack.

Stuart Redmond—He has been working for the Trayborne family for over thirty years. He's protective and faithful, but there are secrets in his past he'd rather forget.

Mildred Redmond—Dr. Martin Trayborne's assistant when he developed NPQ, a neuro-pathway restorative drug that gave Jack his abilities, did she keep the formula secret? Or pass it on before she died?

Benton Redmond—He was whisked off to boarding school at a young age, but now he's back in Black's Cove. What is he looking for?

Ross Morgan—He has the fate of being the only test subject that didn't respond to NPQ. Why?

Chapter One

Olivia Morgan pulled on her lucky red baseball cap, snagged her ponytail and dragged it through the opening in the back. She grabbed off the seat next to her the tool bag containing a lock-pick set, a screwdriver, an extra flashlight and a water bottle.

Sucking in a breath to quiet her nerves, she stared out into the moonlit night at the towering facade of gray granite that housed the Black's Cove Clinic.

Breaking in to obtain her brother's medical file was the only way she'd ever know if their treatment had helped him, or put him in a wheelchair and erased the knowledge of basic human functions from his brain. Her own personal question was why her parents had brought him to this macabre clinic in the first place?

Reaching for the door handle, she pulled it, let the door swing open and climbed out of her car.

The century-old building looked more like a throwback to Elizabethan England than a medical clinic. It was built in the 30's and served as a mental institution until the Trayborne family purchased it in 1956 and converted it into the Black's Cove Clinic.

The hair on the back of her neck rose. She pulled the collar of her jacket up a little closer and eased the car door shut just enough to extinguish the dome light inside. Looping the tool bag strap over her shoulder, she prepared for her assault.

The place had been closed for years, but the newspaper archives she'd been digging through had revealed an interesting fact. The clinic's medical records were still housed in the basement.

Slipping out of the grove of aspens she'd hidden her car in, she walked the edge of the cobbled drive and turned on her mini-flashlight. The skinny beam shone against the weed-laced stones leading up to the gatehouse.

Her hearing went on alert, every muscle in her body firmed in fight-or-flight standby. Why was she so tense? The place was empty. Abandoned. Standing alone in an isolated corner of southeastern Idaho. Getting answers would be like popping in to Jitter's Espresso shop for a latte. Quick and easy.

Pulling resolve from that fact, she stared at the massive structure, its upper floors visible above the eight-foot-high stone wall surrounding it.

A shudder zig-zagged down her spine. She ducked in behind a tall arborvitae, fighting to regain her nerve. She'd taken risks before; it went with her job as a freelance investigative journalist digging for stories on medical mistakes. Ross's condition certainly fit the description.

She swallowed and stepped out from behind the evergreen.

HE KNEW she would come; had seen her in a precognitive vision. And now she was here. Poking around where she didn't belong, searching for answers he'd stop her from finding.

High on the stone wall blended with the tree branches and fall leaves, he watched the faint flicker of her flashlight through the window she'd entered, at the top of the fire escape. Coming to his feet from a squatting position, he willed his physical senses to heighten. Pulling in a deep breath of night air, he dissected its components in his mind, sorting threat from nonthreat in the process. He couldn't sense them, but he knew *they* were here.

Sharpening his eyesight, he dragged his stare through the darkness, coming up empty. Concern fired along his nerves; he had to stop them before they hurt her.

Glancing back at the window, he turned his head slightly to the left, honing in on the sounds coming from the room. He closed his eyes, hearing her hesitant footsteps against the hardwood, the sound of the ancient knob turning, the swish of the door being pulled open and finally the pin sliding into the kick plate as she closed the door and released the knob.

There wasn't much time.

OLIVIA LEANED against the door and shone her flashlight along a corridor to the right. A dead end with a window view. To the left, a long hallway opened up.

Ahead, fifty feet, the light beam bounced off two balusters at the midway point. The stairs, she guessed, glad when she reached them and stared down at the main-floor entrance below.

Six narrow windows rose above the double doors, allowing shards of moonlight to penetrate the interior. The platinum light cut across the great entry hall and illuminated a sitting area, crowded with furniture draped in white covers. Grains of dust danced in and out of the moonbeams, raising the level of caution in her blood.

Had someone stirred it up? Or was she just being paranoid in a dusty old building that made her want to sneeze? She chose the latter and put one foot in front of the other, descending the wide staircase to the ground floor.

She'd give the tip of her right pinky finger for a map of the place, but she'd have to rely on her sense of direction instead. The place had been built at the turn of the century. The kitchen was probably at the back of the building, and so too the stairwell leading to the basement.

Moving off the landing, she turned right, weaving her way through the cloaked furniture. Under the stairwell and directly behind the entry, she found what had once been a dining hall, probably when the building had housed mental patients. It was empty now, save a couple of tables with their chairs upended, legs to the ceiling.

How many patients had dined here?

She picked up her pace through the cavernous room, heading for a row of shutters that lined an opening in the wall to the right. The wide swinging door next to the serving window should lead into the kitchen if she'd guessed right.

Olivia eased the door open, shining the flashlight beam around first before stepping into the massive commercial kitchen. The strong smell of cooking oil and chlorine bleach overwhelmed her nose, almost making her gag.

"Ick," she whispered as she probed the darkness, settling the beam of light on a narrow doorway at the far end of the galley, with a ladder leaned up against it.

"Yes." She moved toward it, a sense of relief stirring in her veins. The sooner she found her brother's file and got the heck out, the better she'd feel. This place gave her the creeps and then some.

She pulled the ladder out of the way, opened the door and stared down the stairwell, pointing the flashlight into the black hole below.

Pulling in a breath, she staved off the desire to turn and run. Down there was the truth and she'd be damned if she was going to stop hunting for it now.

Somewhere in the belly of the structure, a low mechanical groan hummed. About to jump out of her skin, she paused long enough to feel air rush from an overhead vent in the kitchen. The heat had kicked on. Shaking off her jitters, she started down the narrow wooden stairs, her senses on hyperalert.

Every creak of the ancient steps under her feet made her hesitate. At least she'd hear if anyone came down after her. Not that it was even a possibility. She was utterly alone in this place. She hoped.

Olivia reached the bottom of the steps and waved her flashlight around the basement. It had been divided into a series of rooms along the back wall. On her right was a bank of washers and dryers. The clinic's laundry room.

One of the rooms against the wall on the left had to contain the file storage.

Stepping off the landing, she hurried to the first door and pulled it open. Inside was a food pantry, stocked with a smattering of canned goods.

She closed the door and went to the next one. It was locked. This had to be it. Snagging her tool bag off her shoulder, she fished out her lock picking set and knelt in front of the knob. With her light in between her teeth, she inserted the tension bar into the keyhole. Pushing the rake into the lock, above the tension tool, she coaxed the lock pins, feeling them give. The knob turned and she pushed open the door.

Grasping her flashlight, she shone it into the interior of the large room where rows of metal shelves stood as a testament to the number of patients who'd passed through the clinic. Thousands, she guessed. Olivia shoved her tools into the bag, stepped into the room, closed the door behind her and locked it.

She made a quick assessment moving her light around the perimeter. There were no windows.

Turning back toward the door, she focused on the light switch and flipped it on.

Overhead, a couple of incandescent bulbs dangling from shaded pendants came on, casting light down through the tall shelving units arranged in ten rows.

She could only hope each box had been marked with a month and year. It would make finding Ross's medical records a piece of cake, but why her parents had signed a nondisclosure order in the first place, she'd never know. They'd both passed away without giving her the information.

Excitement pulsed in her veins. She turned off the flashlight and slipped it inside her tool bag. In less than ten minutes she'd have the answers she'd guessed at for years.

Staring up at the file boxes, she worked her way up and down the rows, until she spotted a box with the month and year she needed. It was on the top shelf. Frustrated, she moved out of the row, looking for something to climb on. In the corner she spotted a stepladder.

Olivia walked over to it, picked it up and carried it back into the row. She opened the ladder and put her foot on the first rung.

The stairs creaked under someone's weight.

Olivia froze in place, her heartbeat escalating in her own eardrums.

Someone was coming.

A silent curse repeated in her mind as she stepped down off the rung. Whoever was outside the door must know she was in here? If not, the light under the door would be their first clue.

Maybe it was a maintenance man or a…security guard.

She swallowed hard, straining to hear.

There it was again, the groan of the wooden stairs.

Panic ignited in her veins. She went on the defensive. On the right bottom shelf in front of her was an opening between two boxes. She crawled into the void, listening as the doorknob was twisted back and forth a couple of times.

Closing her eyes, she worked to stay calm, pulling air into her lungs in even rhythm.

Overhead, the lights started to buzz, a low-pitched sound, like a bee circling.

A charge of fear racing through her, she opened her eyes and stared up, watching the light overhead dim and glow bright again. A power surge?

Tension held her body captive.

Pop! The glass bulb shattered, sending shards raining to the floor next to her.

A small squeak squeezed from between her lips. She slapped her hand over her mouth.

The second bulb blew into tiny pieces and hit the floor. The room went black.

Olivia reached for her tool bag. The sound of the lock releasing stirred terror in her. It was only a matter of time before she was discovered and arrested.

In desperation, she rummaged in her bag and pulled out the flashlight.

A loud scuffle erupted near the door.

She squeezed the light in her hand, determined to use it as a weapon if anyone got too close.

A deep guttural yell echoed in the room. The sound of mortal combat less than ten feet away from her played out in the dark.

Fear, solid and unmistakable, solidified in her mind.

Something scraped on the floor near her hiding spot. The stepladder she'd left in the row?

It slapped shut, grinding over the floor right past her and splinting into pieces against a wall on the opposite side of the room.

"Where is she?" a raspy male voice demanded from out of the darkness.

"Get out." The order was unmistakable. Olivia strained to see in the blackness, to put a face with the voice, but if she turned on her flashlight, they'd find her for sure.

"Take care of it or we will."

"Don't threaten me."

Bump! Bump! Bump!

All hell broke loose in the room as one by one the shelves banged into each other, falling like dominoes.

She lunged forward in the dark, aiming for a way out before she was caught in the calamity, but she miscalculated her location and slammed into a shelf, hitting her head and losing her ball cap.

Rolling onto her back, she turned on her flashlight just in time to see the first file box careen off the shelf above her.

She rolled to the left to avoid being crushed and ended up on her belly.

A scream rose in her throat.

Squeezing the flashlight as hard as she could, she aimed it toward the door.

There was a hard tug on the flashlight cylinder. Increasing her grip, she hung on to it as tight as she could. Another tug, then a jerk.

The light wrenched from her hand, rocketed across the room, slammed into the wall and went out.

Terror rocked her. What was happening? Who was in the room? Who…or what?

She felt a tiny prick in her right arm through her sleeve and slapped at it. Something clattered to the floor next to her. Patting the cement, her hand came down on a syringe. She'd been drugged?

Fear raced through her as one by one her senses dulled and went into hibernation. Still fighting, she settled into the void and closed her eyes.

"SHE'S DANGEROUS. She'll expose us."

He had to agree, but his methods differed from theirs. "I'll make sure she leaves Black's Cove. Stay away from her. Do you understand?" For emphasis, he mentally shoved them into the wall, holding them there with his mind.

"If you don't get rid of her, we will."

Letting them drop, he stepped back. In an instant, they were gone, leaving him alone in the room with her. The sedative he'd given her would wear off in an hour's time; he could only hope she hadn't seen any of their faces.

Turning in the darkness, he focused on her where she lay between two fallen shelves. She'd been minutes from death. They would have crushed her if he hadn't intervened. But somehow he doubted only intervention was going to be enough to protect Olivia Morgan's life. He'd have to do that and so much more.

Glancing at the file box tipped over next to her, he made a decision. He would allow her to discover enough information about her brother to be satisfied. She would leave Black's Cove and their secret would remain secure.

Moving his hand in front of him, he willed the shelves into place.

They rocked upright, slaves of the telekinetic energy he forced on them. Next the file boxes were raised, refilled and put back into place, all except for the one she was after, that one he mentally slid onto the lowest shelf.

He knew she would return to the clinic in a couple of days—he'd seen it in a precognitive vision. And when she did, she would find what she was looking for.

OLIVIA'S SENSES RETURNED, starting with pain throbbing from a bump on her head. Awareness brought her around and she bolted straight up in the seat, almost banging her forehead on the steering wheel of her car in the process.

What had just happened?

Blinking several times, she got her bearings, shaking off the last of the fog that blanketed her mind. She couldn't recall leaving the clinic. In fact, her last memory was of her flashlight mysteriously being jerked out of her hand.

She swallowed, fishing for memories beyond that. Nothing. Still, she couldn't keep a shudder at bay. It ripped through her, setting her nerves on end.

"Dang." She hadn't gotten the file. Reaching up she patted her naked head. Her lucky red ball cap was missing. She'd dropped a clue, but she wasn't going back for it tonight.

Turning the key in the ignition, she started her car and glanced at the clock on the dashboard. It was 3:20 a.m. She was missing an hour? She eyed the clinic as she pulled out into the driveway.

She had to have Ross's file. She'd be back to try again, but next time, she'd come prepared for whatever lurked in the basement.

STEPPING OUT of the woods, he stared at the taillights of her car in the distance. He could still smell her sweet floral scent on the red baseball cap in his hand and on his clothes, still see the curve of her face as he'd carried her to her car and put her safely inside.

A wave of indignation raged through him. Olivia Morgan had to leave Black's Cove. He wouldn't have her blood on his hands.

He'd been watching her every move, but so had the others. They'd followed her here tonight just like he had. That knowledge worried him as he stepped out of cover and onto the cobblestone path that led him away from the building and all the secrets it contained.

Chapter Two

Olivia sat in a booth next to the window in the local coffee shop on Main Street. Her unobstructed view of the front door of *Black's Cove Gazette* made the cup of weak coffee sitting in front of her almost palatable.

The newspaper would open in ten minutes. She glanced at her list, information she had to dig up from the newspaper's archives.

A racy black Jaguar pulled up to the curb next to the restaurant. A man climbed out of the car, pausing long enough to lock the vehicle.

She gave him a once-over, sure he was the best looking thing she'd seen in this town to date. She stared at his broad shoulders as he turned, jaywalked across the street and disappeared into the *Gazette* office.

"Refill?" the waitress asked, holding a half-full coffeepot in her hand.

"Sure." Olivia slid her cup to the edge of the table. "That's a pretty great car, don't you think?"

Glancing up at the young woman, she held her breath.

The ploy was lame, but if it got her a name, then the benign question was worth it.

"That's Jack Trayborne's car. You should see his red convertible."

"I bet it's even better." She pulled her full cup back and reached for the sugar. *So this was the infamous Jack Trayborne?* "He's easy on the eyes, too. Is he single?"

The waitress's cheeks pinked and she was about to reply, when an older woman waved at her from behind the counter. "Your order's up, Emily."

She nodded and turned around.

Olivia smiled to herself, pretty sure the young woman was nursing a crush. She could almost do the same, if she didn't think Jack Trayborne was hiding secrets.

She had half a mind to march over to the *Gazette* and confront him face to face, but taunting the tiger before the cage door was all the way shut could get you bit. She loved risk, but not risk without a cause.

After last night's freaky encounter in the basement of the clinic, she planned to lay low, blend in, ask the locals about Trayborne and hope to get some answers that would put her investigation back on track. Because at the moment, she didn't have squat.

The front door of the newspaper office pushed open and he stepped out onto the sidewalk.

Olivia focused on his dark good looks, enjoying the way the morning sun glinted off his coffee-colored hair. He was decked out in a charcoal gray business suit and much younger than she expected, midthirties she guessed. He didn't look like a threat, but she couldn't keep a sense of foreboding from coasting over her nerves.

An elderly couple paused to speak with him. He smiled at something they said, nodding his head in agreement. They waved before moving down the street, arm in arm.

Jack Trayborne crossed the road, a hint of a smile still bowing his sexy mouth. He reached his car, pausing next to it to raise his cell phone to his ear. He glanced over the car's roof as he spoke, meeting her gaze with deep blue eyes and a placid expression.

A jolt of attraction zapped her. Her throat constricted and the heat of embarrassment rushed into her cheeks.

She broke the connection first and picked up her cup, bringing it to her lips in a nonchalant manner she didn't feel. He'd set her damn nerves on fire and she was blowing it. There wasn't much incognito about gawking at her enemy.

Chancing another look, she almost choked. In the instant between realization and reality, he'd slipped away.

She set down the cup, tossed a couple of bucks on the table and left the café.

Looking both ways, she crossed the street and entered the *Gazette*, determined to forget about the odd encounter. This was one strange town; it only stood to reason that Jack Trayborne was odd, too.

"Miss Morgan," the receptionist said, looking up from behind a high counter positioned between the public and the newsroom, visible behind a half wall of glass. "How can I help you?"

"I'd like to use the archives for a couple of hours this morning."

"I'm sorry, that's not possible."

A zing of caution wiggled up her spine. "Is there a problem?" She glanced at the sign-in sheet on the counter. It was blank.

"No. No problem. The exterminator is coming in to spray this morning. Everything has been draped. No one is allowed down there right now."

Arguing didn't appear to be an option. Anyway, who could argue for exposure to chemicals.

"When can I get into the archives?" she asked, picking up the morning's edition of the newspaper from the desk. The headline leaped out at her. Phantom Saves Elderly Couple from Plunge off Hwy 21.

Couple claims they never saw the man who saved their lives, but they don't dispute that the phantom played a role in their miraculous rescue and they believe he exists....

"At the end of the week."

"Hmm?" She snapped back into the conversation, still pondering the ridiculous article.

"I'll come back then. Thanks." Olivia put the newspaper down, turned and left the office, pausing on the sidewalk to get her irritation under control before she crossed the street again and headed for her car. Up until this point, the *Gazette* had been her only source of information. She'd used archived articles to establish a time line on the clinic and its nefarious activities, but she still had to obtain Ross's medical file.

An involuntary shiver crept over her body and bloomed on her skin as goose bumps. If she had an explanation for what had happened last night she'd feel better, but the unknown aspects left her nerves in tatters. Things definitely went bump in the night around here.

Had she simply walked to her car and climbed in without being aware? It didn't make sense, but neither did any of the things that had taken place in that creepy basement.

Strolling at an easy pace, she headed for her vehicle.

In the distance, a siren howled and a police cruiser whizzed past, lights flashing. It turned right onto a side street.

Somehow, the commotion seemed out of place in the sleepy town of five thousand residents, where everyone seemed to know everyone else.

Curiosity zipped through her. The police car was headed in the same direction as her hotel.

Picking up her pace, she reached her car, pulled her keys out of her pocket and climbed in. She fired the engine and pulled out onto the main drag.

At the intersection of Main and 10th, one block up, she took a left, then another, finally turning onto 9th street, headed for her hotel. Up ahead, she spotted flashing emergency lights.

Caution stirred in her blood. They looked like they were corralled in front of her hotel.

Olivia pushed down on the gas pedal, an extension of her need to get to the scene as soon as possible.

She pulled into the parking lot on the side of the Emory Hotel and climbed out of her car. Moving quickly, she entered the main entrance, noting a couple of officers standing at the front desk speaking with the clerk. There didn't appear to be anything urgent going on. She headed for the elevator. Lights and sirens usually spelled trouble for someone.

The elevator glided to a stop, illuminating the number 4 above the door before it dinged and the doors slid open.

Olivia exited into the hallway and stopped. At the end of the corridor two more uniformed officers milled around, another cop with a notepad appeared to be questioning a guest. Realization slammed into her brain at the same moment she charged down the hall.

An officer looked up. "You can't come in here, miss. We're investigating a break-in."

"It's my room!"

He stepped back, motioning her inside.

Olivia walked through the open door, almost running into another cop who was snapping pictures with a digital camera.

"What happened?" she asked, staring at the interior of the hotel room she'd occupied for the last five days. Worry laced through her as she looked for her laptop in the upheaval.

They got my laptop?

"This is your room?" the officer asked, turning his attention on her.

"Yeah." Olivia swallowed, staring in disbelief at the chaos someone had inflicted on the place. The mattress was ripped open, stuffing scattered on the floor like puffy clouds. Dresser drawers were yanked out, her clothes tossed in every direction. One of the two lamps in the room lay smashed on the floor. The place was uninhabitable.

"Did you have valuables, miss?"

"Olivia Morgan."

"Miss Morgan."

"My laptop. Nothing else really matters." Caution latched on to her nerves. She stepped to the window, pulled back the drapes and stared down into the parking lot.

Whoever broke in knew she wasn't in her room. Was she being followed?

At the back entrance of the lot, she caught a glimpse of black, just in time to see Jack Trayborne's Jaguar turn right out of the parking lot and jettison away.

Anger sluiced in her veins, but she held her tongue. Was it possible he'd trashed her room and stolen her laptop? It did contain her research and the makings of her exposé about the Black's Cove Clinic. Information that could eventually convict the Trayborne Foundation and the clinic for medical mistakes.

"Any idea how they got in?"

"We're going to dust for prints, but because the window is fixed, we believe the perpetrator came in through the door."

"My laptop is a Mac. I have the serial number written down at home. I'll have to phone it in to you after I leave."

"Anything else?"

"No. I can probably salvage my clothes and personal items."

The officer scribbled on a police report. "Do you know of anyone who might have reason to break into your room?"

Jack Trayborne. "No. I've been in town for less than a week. I don't know anyone, really."

"Okay, Miss Morgan. We'll do what we can to catch the perpetrator and recover your laptop. Do you have a cell phone number where we can reach you?"

Olivia rattled off her number and turned toward the door. "I'm going to get another room. I'll stop by later to collect my things."

The officer nodded and she stepped out into the hallway, striding past an officer questioning a hotel guest. The man appeared to be more agitated with each question the officer posed.

"Excuse me." Olivia moved past them only half listening to the exchange.

"I'm not crazy. I know what I saw!" The exasperated man's raised voice sliced into her nerves and tuned her hearing. Her steps faltered and she purposely slowed to a crawl, listening over her shoulder.

"The door was wide open. I looked in and the damn mattress was sailing off the bed! There was no one in that room, Officer. No one at all."

Olivia stopped in front of the elevator, fighting a wave of anxiety that couldn't be contained. He wasn't crazy. She wasn't crazy, even though she felt a little nuts when she replayed the odd things that went on last night at the clinic.

The elevator chimed and the doors slid open. She stepped inside and pushed the button for the lobby. The doors glided closed and she tried to relax, but every muscle in her body had other ideas.

What if she'd been followed here? Caution laced through her. Maybe she should change hotels. But what good would it do? Maybe she was better off staying put. The security in the hotel would be ramped up now that there had been a break-in.

The elevator reached the lobby level, the doors opened and she walked to the front desk.

"Hi."

A starched-looking woman in a white blouse and tailored blue jacket instantly smiled at her.

"Miss Morgan. We're so sorry about the break-in. We carry insurance. Perhaps you'd like to fill out a form for the replacement of any items that were stolen?"

"Yeah. I'd like that. But right now, I need another room."

"I'll see what's available." The woman moved to her computer.

Olivia leaned on the counter, listening to the clack of the keys.

"You've been booked into the Presidential Suite on the sixth floor."

She straightened. "Really. By whom?"

"The owner, Miss Morgan."

"And who would that be?"

"Jack Trayborne."

Anger sizzled in her veins and she nearly let out a growl.

"That's very nice of Mr. Trayborne." She pasted a smile on her lips. Was Jack Trayborne aware of her mission in Black's Cove? She certainly had to consider the possibility that she'd been found out. Maybe the receptionist at the *Gazette* had ratted her out and told him about her long hours in the dusty archives. Maybe he was the one who'd destroyed her room and taken her laptop to see how far she'd gotten?

"He came as soon as the manager alerted him to what had happened. He's extremely sorry your security was compromised and requests that you have carte blanche, beginning with the suite."

The phone call she'd seen him take in front of the coffee shop?

A measure of resolve soothed her irate nerves. Was it a ploy to placate her with creature comforts? Or a genuine gesture? She couldn't be sure. "That won't be necessary. I'll take another standard room, please."

The woman's eyes widened. "Are you sure, Miss Morgan?"

"Yes." She couldn't keep her foot from tapping against the thick carpet in front of the desk. She wouldn't be put off the scent by his goodwill. She knew plenty of his type. Money didn't buy character.

"Here you are, room 304." She handed her the key card. "If you change your mind, be sure to let us know."

Olivia took the key. "Thank you, but this will do."

She nodded and headed for the elevator, more determined than before to find out what Jack Trayborne was hiding at the Black's Cove Clinic, a curiosity she planned to satisfy tonight no matter how terrifying she found that damn basement.

OLIVIA STARED INTO FOG as thick as her Grandma Edna's gravy. She couldn't see five feet in front of her as she shone her flashlight down at the cobble drive leading up to the gatehouse.

It was like a bad rerun; worse the second time around. The only saving factor was, if she couldn't see, she couldn't be seen.

She reached the gatehouse and found the gate wide open. Moisture coated her sweatshirt, its dampness reaching clear down to her bones. She shivered as she pushed through the gate, aiming for the shadow of the clinic she could almost make out in the mist.

She planned to use the same window to enter, if it hadn't been closed and locked. The thought put a measure of worry in her head. What if she couldn't get the file?

Olivia shook off the notion as she reached the right side of the building. She hurried along the side and around the back corner, pausing only once to get her bearings.

Breathing deeply, she pulled the earthy scent of the fog deep into her lungs.

Pushing on, she scaled the fire escape and climbed through the window she'd used before. Relief worked through her. Things were going so easily.

Too easily?

She straightened and pulled her Taser out of her tool bag. This time, she'd come prepared to defend herself. From whom or what, she didn't know, but she didn't plan to lose an entire hour of her life again in some unknown scenario.

Weapon ready and flashlight showing the way, she pulled open the door and stepped out into the hallway. She reached the staircase and took the steps two at a time. Breezing through the sitting area and the dining room, she didn't slow until she reached the swinging door that led into the kitchen.

Easing it open, she mentally prepared for the stench of oil and bleach. She stepped through the door and let it swing behind her.

She hurried through the galley and down the stairs, anxious to get in and get out. The door into the storage room stood open. She pulled up short and shone her light around the interior.

"Damn." The place had been cleaned up. Even the towering metal shelves were in the upright position, not an easy task judging by their size. Certainly whoever had put the place back together knew there'd been some kind of fight down here. Had they increased security?

A zap of caution jolted her and she instantly listened for any sounds of pursuit.

Nothing.

Stepping into the room, she reached for the light switch and flipped it on, surprised that even the bulbs had been replaced, but she didn't extinguish her flashlight this time.

Easing along the rows, she found the one where she'd discovered the file box she wanted. Raising the light beam to the uppermost shelf, she searched for the box. It was gone.

Dread shot holes in her resolve. Was it possible whoever had been in the room that night took the information? Was it possible someone knew what she was after?

About to give up, Olivia glanced down, the edge of her beam flicking over a file box on the lowest shelf.

Her heart rate kicked up. She dropped to her knees and reached for the box. She swallowed and put her Taser down on the floor, then the flashlight.

It was her lucky day…night, she decided as she pulled the lid off the box. The light penetration from overhead was negligible and she picked up the flashlight, sticking it between her teeth and aiming it into the box as she flipped through the files one by one.

They weren't alphabetized, something that would have saved her time.

Silently, she repeated the names on the files until she reached the one with "Morgan, Ross A" printed on the tab.

Olivia's breath clogged in her lungs, whether a result of the dusty files or the emotion choking her throat, she wasn't sure, but one thing was for certain, she'd found what she was looking for.

Slowly, she opened the file and pulled the flashlight out of her mouth, focusing its beam on the faded typewritten pages, paper clipped to the inside of the manila folder.

There was the standard information—height, weight, blood pressure, pulse rate, patient I.D. She studied the sketch of a human foot with three small dots on it in a triangular pattern. Frustrated, she flipped up the first page of the three-page file, looking for the doctor's notes, the diagnosis, anything that would tell her what sort of treatment he'd received in the clinic.

Her eyes focused on a paragraph written in long hand. It was barely legible, but she muddled through, soaking in the information.

The patient has irreversible brain damage, which appears to be nonresponsive to treatment at this time. I administered a 200cc dose of NPQ, but the patient remained in an unresponsive state. At this time, we have done everything we can for him.

This couldn't be all there was to Ross's file. There had to be more.

The click of the light switch startled her. She quickly closed the file and raised her flashlight beam toward the door, determined to meet the threat head-on this time.

With her free hand, she slid the file into her tool bag and looped it over her shoulder. Picking up the Taser, she stood up, prepared for battle.

The door slammed shut.

She jumped, watching in horror and awe, as an eight-foot desk skidded past on its own and jammed against the door, trapping her inside.

Terror exploded in her body. She bolted forward.

Was she losing her mind?

Panic took hold of her. She lunged for the desk and tried to shove it away from the exit. It wouldn't budge. Some unseen force held it in place.

The hiss of a match somewhere in the room sent a shot of terror into her heart.

The unmistakable odor of sulfur filled the air.

She watched in shock as a pile of papers in the corner of the room ignited and flames raced up the wall.

Caustic smoke filled the enclosed room, invading her lungs, burning her eyes. Her throat squeezed shut.

Dropping to the floor next to the desk, she pulled the tool bag off her shoulder and yanked off her sweatshirt. Digging into her bag, she took out the bottle of water she always carried and doused the sweatshirt.

Holding the wet cloth to her nose as a filter, she stood and tried again to push the desk out of the way, but it was useless.

Reality choked out any hope she had left as she began to feel the dizzying effects of the toxic smoke.

Sinking down onto the floor, she conserved her strength for another attempt.

If she didn't get out in the next minute, she was as good as dead.

Chapter Three

He could hear the thump of her heartbeat through the door. She was still alive, but she wouldn't be for long if he didn't get inside.

Raising his hand out in front of him, he pushed against the door, feeling the resistance holding it shut. What had they done?

Pulling in a deep breath, he focused all his energy on the object behind the door and felt it give, a little at first, before he heard it grind across the floor.

The door opened with a violent crack, hitting against the doorstop.

Smoke belched from the room, setting off the fire alarm.

He covered his mouth and nose and charged in, spotting her next to the massive desk that had been used to lock her in.

Luckily, they hadn't stayed to make sure their sick plan worked. He pulled her into his arms, raced out of the room and up the stairs. He carried her through the dining hall, the entryway and out the front door.

The alarm would bring the fire department. She couldn't be found at the scene.

Fog blanketed the landscape as he moved along the walkway, headed for the gatehouse. He couldn't let her see his face, but he needed to make sure she was okay.

Carrying her into the woods next to the driveway, he found a clearing in the trees and carefully put her down on the grass.

There were no soot markings around her nose or mouth. No indication that she suffered from smoke inhalation.

Reaching down, he brushed his hand against her cheek. She flinched. She was breathing normally. Still, he couldn't be certain why she appeared to be unconscious.

Was it possible she'd faked the condition?

Focusing his energy, he reached into her mind and caught her stream of thought. She was waiting. Waiting for the precise moment to open her eyes and catch him looking down at her. She wanted to discover his identity.

In a flash, he jumped to his feet, turned and took a leap into the fog.

OLIVIA SAT UP as fast as she could, but she wasn't quick enough. She could just make out the shadow of someone retreating into the mist through the trees.

Dammit. Once again, she'd been rescued by a faceless someone…or…something. But this time she was extremely grateful.

In the distance she heard the wail of sirens, no doubt headed to the fire in the basement of the clinic.

Patting her shoulder, she let out a groan and stood up. Her tool bag was missing. The file she'd just risked her life to retrieve was probably burned to a crisp by now.

Disappointment chewed through her. At least she'd been able to read the first paragraph written by the doctor. It had revealed what she'd always known. Ross had irreversible brain damage. But what was NPQ? She'd have to plug the letters into a computer somewhere to see if she could pull up any results. And the patient I.D., she was certain she'd seen those marks on Ross's left ankle. Beyond that, she had nothing.

Carefully, she pushed through the trees and tried to figure out where she was. The smell of smoke hung in the mist and the fire roared in the distance.

Stumbling forward, she came out at the edge of the cobbled drive. She took a left, following the stones until she reached her car.

The hum of the fire trucks drew closer and she climbed into her car to wait.

The flash of lights against the fog bathed her hiding spot in waves of red. One fire engine rolled past, then another.

Olivia started her car, put it in Drive and eased out of the aspen grove. The bump of the stones under her tires was comforting. She'd be safely out of here in a minute or so and headed back to town with new information. It did seem like they'd tried to help Ross at the clinic.

A measure of doubt crept into her mind. If the clinic had only attempted to cure Ross and hadn't worsened his already-devastating condition, then there was nothing for her to expose. Still, the Trayborne Foundation had set up a trust fund for him. Why would they do something like that if they had no guilt in making him worse?

The glow of headlights in front of her came up so fast that she barely had time to slam on her brakes and pull the steering wheel hard to the right.

A black Jaguar whipped past on the left.

Olivia glanced in her rearview mirror and saw his brake lights come on in the mist.

It made sense that Jack Trayborne would show up here. It was, after all, his facility.

But she couldn't let him identify her.

Stepping down on the gas pedal, she launched forward, keeping the car in between the trees that lined both sides of the road. Had he seen her car well enough to identify it?

He would certainly be asking questions about who had started the fire. Just the memory of watching the blaze erupt with no one around made her skin crawl. Maybe it had been started by spontaneous combustion? Maybe there were oily rags in the corner? But no matter how hard she tried to explain away what she'd seen tonight, she couldn't.

Something strange was going on at the Black's Cove Clinic. Something terrifying and otherworldly. Something she didn't want to believe.

Not even for a moment.

OLIVIA SAT IN ONE of a dozen Internet cubicles in the Black's Cove Community Library.

Her hands shook as she typed the letters *NPQ* into the search engine and pressed Enter.

The screen filled with possible matches. One by one she scanned them, eliminating each result until her gaze settled on one interpretation of the acronym.

Neuro Pathway Quotient...Neuro Pathway Quotient.

She wasn't a doctor, but she knew enough about brain injuries to know it destroyed neuro pathways.

She clicked on the link and an article about the subject popped up on screen. It had been included as reference material in a medical research paper dated May 1999. The copyright on the source paper was 1979, pre-Internet.

A rush of excitement charged through her. The copyright holder was Martin J. Trayborne, the patriarch of the Black's Cove Clinic. Jack Trayborne's grandfather.

Olivia selected the print option and sent the request. In the background, she heard the laser printer fire up as she scanned the article.

A lot of medical jargon filled the page, but a single paragraph caught her attention.

I have managed to isolate the protein responsible for the formation of new neuro pathways. I am hopeful that this discovery will result in the formation of new attachments within the patient's injured brain, rewiring and resetting the synapses.

Was this why her parents had brought Ross to the clinic? For some sort of miracle cure? It was a heroic effort, but obviously, it had failed. She swallowed and sat back in her chair. If Ross was used as a human guinea pig, were there others?

Was there any way to get at the Foundation's financial records? If Ross had a trust account, then maybe others had been established, as well.

A loud screech interrupted Olivia's thoughts.

She spun around in the swivel chair, her brain trying to process what her eyes were seeing.

Paper shot out of the holding tray on the printer, like fast balls off a pitcher's glove.

The librarian scrambled, trying to shut off the kamikaze machine.

Olivia stood up and rushed to help. Finding the power cord plugged into the floor, she pulled it. The printer ground to a stop.

What on earth was happening? she wondered as she turned back to her computer cube, only to find her screen and every other monitor had gone black.

"Oh my, there must have been a power surge of some sort," the librarian said as she crawled around on the floor picking up the paper.

"Has this ever happened before?"

"Not to my knowledge."

Olivia knelt next to the flustered woman and helped her scoot the sheets into a pile.

"I was printing out an article I found on the Internet. Did you happen to see it?"

"No," she continued to work the mess into a neat stack. "Everything here is blank."

Olivia placed the last piece of paper on the stack and

stood up. Glancing around the library, she studied the two lone patrons. A young teenaged girl and a middle-aged woman. Neither of them looked like a would-be printer-monger and Internet saboteur.

This freaky episode was too much like what she'd experienced in the basement of the clinic. Otherworldly.

"Thanks. I'll come back when the Internet is up."

The librarian tucked a stray strand of gray hair back behind her ear and nodded. "Thanks for your help."

"You're welcome." She exited the single-story library building and stepped out onto the sidewalk. Scanning the street in both directions, she half expected to see Jack Trayborne's distinctive car, but it wasn't there. How was it he always seemed to be nearby when things got weird?

Maybe it was time to poke the tiger.

She watched an older gentleman move toward her on the sidewalk.

"Excuse me, sir."

He stopped, a polite smile on his mouth. "Yes, can I help you?"

"I need directions. Can you tell me where I might find Jack Trayborne's home?"

His smile vanished. "No, I'm sorry, I don't know where he lives." The man hurried away, leaving her amused.

Surely someone like Jack Trayborne was well-known in the community his family established. She'd almost bet everyone in town knew who he was and where he lived.

"Excuse me." She stopped an elderly woman with a shopping bag on her arm. "Can you tell me where I might find Jack Trayborne's home?"

The woman shook her head and picked up her pace in an effort to get away.

His address wasn't listed in the phone book; she'd already checked. Maybe she could find out where he lived through the hotel?

About to give up, she spotted a young woman pushing a stroller along the sidewalk. It was worth another try.

"Excuse me, miss."

The woman stopped. "Yes?"

"I was wondering if you know who Jack Trayborne is?"

An instant smile spread on her lips. "Yes, I do. In fact, he's my hero."

Her confusion must have amplified on her face, because the young woman attempted to clarify.

"He saved Gracie's life."

"Gracie?"

"My baby girl."

Olivia's heart nearly pounded out of her chest. Staring down, she looked at the baby tucked into her stroller in a fluffy pink blanket. She had her mother's pretty brown eyes.

"He saved your little girl? From what?"

"An out of control car. We were on the corner of Main and 11th. Grace was in her stroller. Virginia Radcliff accidently hit the gas pedal instead of her brake when the light turned red. She lost control of her car. It came through the intersection and jumped the curb. Jack Trayborne grabbed me and Gracie and pushed us out of the way. The car ended up right where we'd been waiting to cross. If it hadn't been for him, we wouldn't be here." She looked down at her baby and the little girl smiled up at her mother.

Olivia could see how much she loved her child and a measure of respect for Jack Trayborne took shape in her brain.

"That's a touching story, with a happy ending. I was wondering if you can tell me where he lives."

"It's easy to find. It's just west of Black's Cove Clinic."

An ounce of dread leaked from her bones and splayed across her nerves. She'd made a silent vow to avoid that place like the plague.

Leaning over, she stared down at the adorable baby girl, pursed her lips, and made a clicking sound. Gracie responded, a toothless grin pulling up her mouth and bunching her baby cheeks. "Bye-bye, sweetie, glad you're safe, and thank you…" She glanced at Gracie's mom.

"Judy…Judy Bartholomew."

"Judy. Maybe I'll see you again."

The young mother nodded and continued along the sidewalk.

Olivia pulled in a breath and headed for her hotel four blocks away. She planned to return to the library for a copy of the article she'd found on the Internet, but for now, she needed to write down everything she'd discovered about NPQ. And then there was Jack Trayborne. Hero, rescuer of women and infants. A Black's Cove resident everyone had to know, but wouldn't talk about or betray. Why?

Could she risk a face-to-face meeting with him before she'd uncovered enough ammunition to counter the verbal assault she was sure he'd launch against her and her exposé?

CAUTION WORKED its way through him as he stood in the deep shadows next to the street watching her speak briefly with Judy Bartholomew. Turning his head slightly, he searched for the sound of her voice among the street noise, picking out enough of the conversation to understand the trouble it invoked. After a couple of moments, she resumed her stroll along the sidewalk on the opposite side.

Olivia Morgan hadn't left well enough alone, hadn't taken the information from the clinic and come to a conclusion that would have made her leave town singing the praises of the facility's attempts to help her brother. To give him a normal life.

Everything was in danger as long as she remained here. Her life, the lives of anyone who dared to help her along the way and his secret. Their secret.

Worry ground over his nerves and forced him into the sunlight. The air was charged; he could feel the surge of energy on his skin. He searched for a source, isolating it to within a block of where he stood. They were up to something.

Picking out Olivia's movements, he reached out and put a field of protection around her.

The squeal of brakes behind him brought his head around.

An out-of-control sedan zoomed past, the driver waving his hands frantically.

Turning back around, he saw Olivia crossing the street one block ahead of him.

He broke into a run.

They planned to kill her, had from the moment she'd stepped foot in Black's Cove. In that instant, he realized how determined they were to keep their secret. He wanted to keep it, too, but at the expense of another human being's life?

He heard the impact, felt it jar his bones much like it jarred hers.

Bolting in between a couple of cars, he ground to a stop, assessing the situation unfolding at the intersection less than fifty feet away.

Heightening his senses, he listened for her heartbeat among the crowd gathering around the spot where Olivia Morgan lay in the street. There were too many of them to isolate her distinctive cardiac rhythm.

Concern pushed him forward. He mixed with the growing mass of interested folks who wanted to catch a glimpse of what had happened.

The hair at his nape bristled, warning him they were nearby, watching just like he was. Waiting, hoping, praying their brutal attempt to deal with Olivia Morgan had succeeded this time.

Chapter Four

Olivia faded in and out of consciousness, wondering where it hurt, if it hurt and what had just happened.

She opened her eyes, staring up at the crowd gathered around her. The asphalt under her was hard and cold. She'd been hit by a car? It was the only thing that made sense.

The sudden pressure of hands on her body sent a charge of electricity shooting through her along with disbelief as she tried to sit up, realizing there was no one next to her.

She closed her eyes again, trying to reason away what was happening. It was crazy. Maybe she was unconscious or imagining the feel of hands moving over her body, almost like an examination. As quickly as the odd sensation took her, it stopped.

Sucking in a breath, she sat up, focusing on the faces of the people crowding around her.

"Hurry! Someone call an ambulance. I think she's hurt." A man in his twenties knelt next to her and touched her arm. "Are you okay?" he asked in an excited voice.

She stared at him and nodded her head. "I think so." Mentally she searched for any injuries, but short of feeling slightly dizzy and a bit out of sync, nothing else hurt.

"It knocked the wind out of me and I banged my head on the pavement." Reaching up, she touched a tender spot on her left temple, and recoiled in pain.

The wail of sirens screamed in the distance, but she found her hearing focused on a voice in the throng of people.

"The Phantom protected her." The whispered comment drew a string of agreement through the crowd.

The Phantom? Protection? The people in this town were certifiable, she decided. This was a simple case of car versus pedestrian, and the car hadn't won. Just like the elderly couple had been lucky and escaped their accident.

Olivia attempted to stand up, but nausea pushed her back down. She fought off a rush of panic. She didn't want to go to the hospital. She hated hospitals. But maybe she did need to be checked out.

The sirens grew louder and finally quit about the time the crowd parted and a couple of EMTs carrying equipment stepped through the crowd and knelt next to her.

"What happened?" the EMT asked, opening his jump kit.

Olivia focused on his name tag. Todd Nicholls. At least she was still cognitive.

"I'm fine. The car barely touched me. Nothing is broken." She searched for the vehicle, her stare settling on the crushed bumper that hung at a cockeyed angle from the impact.

A measure of disbelief tingled in the back of her brain. She should be hurt. If the condition of the car was any indication, she should be broken, but she wasn't.

"I don't need to go to the hospital." A wave of claustrophobia washed over her and she closed her eyes for a moment until it passed. When she opened them again, she was ready to stand up.

"You took a terrific hit, Miss. We'd feel better if you got checked over in the ER."

A measure of reason silenced her protest and she nodded. "You're right. I don't feel so great. Better safe than sorry."

One of the medics went to retrieve the gurney and she watched him maneuver it through the masses being slowly pushed back by a uniformed officer, as his partner questioned the driver.

"Nothing to see here, folks. Move along, let the medics work."

Glancing up, her gaze locked on the only familiar face in the crowd. *Jack Trayborne?* She'd know his intense blue eyes anywhere, but before she could decipher the look of anger on his face, he stepped back into the throng.

An unexplained jolt of disappointment glanced off her brain. What had she hoped would happen? That he'd rush to her side and begin a conversation? Spill the clinic's secrets in the middle of the street next to her?

A slingshot full of reality slammed into her brain, leaving her almost giddy in its simplicity.

She'd been digging down the wrong tunnel, mining the clinic's secrets, when she needed to be uncovering his. He was Black's Cove Clinic.

Olivia tried to relax as the EMTs wrapped her up like a mummy in a C-collar and strapped her to a back-board. It was all for the sake of *her* safety in the event she'd injured her spine in the accident, but that didn't help her level of discomfort as they wheeled her into the ambulance and headed for the hospital.

RAGE CONSUMED HIM as he took the steps two at a time, his heart pounding out a war beat he was sure they'd heard long before he kicked open the door in the empty warehouse loft and stepped into the dark room.

Waves of energy rushed him, but he encircled himself in a wall of protection much like the one he'd used to save Olivia's life in the street below.

Reaching into the darkness with his mind, he found them standing together in the corner. The mental contact solidified their involvement, as he pulled in their thoughts.

Fear, slow to take shape but palpable, emanated from one of them, but the other…

"I said I'd deal with her. She's mine! Do you understand?"

"You've had enough time. We won't stop until you get rid of her."

Anger streamed through him like molten lava. It hit its flashpoint in a violent explosion he couldn't imme-diately control.

"No!" He thrust out his hand in front of him, sending them into the wall. The interior of the warehouse reverberated with the impact and he watched them both hit the ground in a crumpled heap.

Pulling huge gulps of air into his lungs, his rage dissipated. He stepped toward them.

Going to his knees, he rolled them both over, satisfied when they stirred and sat up.

"If you touch her again, you won't survive. Do I make myself clear?"

Begrudgingly, they both nodded, rubbing various parts of their bodies, still throbbing from the impact, but he had to be sure. Reaching into their minds, he listened to their stream of thought, satisfied that Olivia Morgan was safe for the time being.

He came to his feet, feeling drained, and left the loft. He had to protect her. Perhaps the time had come to force her into his arms, but from what he knew about her, she wasn't going to come quietly.

OLIVIA STARED straight ahead, while the ER doctor shone a light in her eyes, first one, then the other.

He stepped back and shoved his hands in the pockets of his lab coat. "You've got a mild concussion. No broken bones. I'd say you're a lucky lady."

"Thanks. Now, when can I get out of here?"

"I'll sign off on the discharge papers, but you need to follow this tip sheet on head injuries. If you experience any of the symptoms, you need to return to the hospital immediately."

"Okay." Olivia reached out and took the diagnostic paper from the doctor. "If I have any trouble, I promise I'll come back."

He left through the curtain surrounding the cubical, and she slowly got dressed. She did feel like she'd gone a couple of rounds with a prize fighter. Tomorrow morning was going to be a bear. That's when the bruises would show up in an ugly shade of purple. She could already feel the asphalt burns on her cheek, forearm and elbow.

But what the hell had really happened in the middle of the street? The truth was, she should be in the ICU, but she wasn't.

She swallowed hard, trying to figure it out as she pulled on her blouse. It was almost as if some unseen force was standing between her and the speeding car. A wall, a barrier of some sort. A chill wiggled through her and she couldn't deny its source. Fear. She'd only been in Black's Cove for a solid week and she'd almost been killed twice. Most sane individuals would run screaming from this strange town.

She was screaming, but she didn't plan to run.

Olivia pulled on her shoes and tied them. Folding the paperwork, she shoved it into the back pocket of her jeans and pushed back the privacy curtain.

The ER hummed with activity. Nurses scampered around, medical equipment in hand. It was hard not to feel the rising level of tension in the air.

Focusing on the set of double doors at the end of the corridor, she headed for the exit, but the sound of emergency tones caught her attention. She slowed her pace.

"BC ER, unit three. We're en route with an unresponsive female patient. Name Judy Bartholomew, age twenty-four, possible suicide attempt by ingestion. We're ten minutes out if we beat the AOT 11:55 freight into town."

A train whistle, distinct and unmistakable came in over the emergency vehicles's radio frequency and Olivia deciphered the acronym AOT, always on time.

The nurse pressed the button on the microphone. "Copy unit three, we'll be waiting. Any information on the drug she took?"

"Negative. We found a couple of pills next to her on the bed, but no bottle. We're bringing them in for analysis. Unit three clear."

"BC hospital, clear." The nurse turned and headed for one of the trauma bays at the rear of the ER, shouting the information. "Female patient, age twenty-four…"

Olivia wanted to cup her hands over her ears to shut it out. She'd spoken to Judy Bartholomew just over an hour ago about where Jack Trayborne lived. She'd been the only one willing to give her any information. The image of Gracie staring up at her mother flashed in her mind, followed by a wave of disbelief that threatened to overwhelm her. She reached out and sagged against the wall.

"Miss Morgan? Are you all right?"

"I'm fine, I just need to sit down for a moment." She spotted a chair near the end of the hall and headed for it, with a nurse next to her.

"Do you need to see Doctor Rawlings again?"

"No. I'll be fine. I just need to sit."

"I'll be back to check on you in a few minutes."

"Thanks." She watched Nurse Jackson join the others, busy preparing for their critical patient.

Olivia closed her eyes, but couldn't get the image of Judy and Gracie out of her mind. What did a suicidal person look like anyway? Had Judy been wearing the signs right under her nose? Did her smile and friendly help only mask a deep-seated problem?

She didn't want to believe she'd attempted to kill herself, but she really didn't know her.

Flashing red and white strobe lights reflected off the walls of the ambulance bay in a dizzying cycle.

Tension squeezed every muscle in Olivia's body until she thought she'd suffocate. She bolted to her feet, watching the ambulance doors swing open and the gurney roll out, assisted by a couple of EMTs.

Right behind them a man climbed out holding a baby girl. Gracie. He must be Judy's husband.

Olivia's heart squeezed and she searched for air, pulling a haggard breath into her lungs. The uncertainty and fear he must be feeling was etched in deep lines across his forehead.

She stepped back against the wall to avoid being in the way as the ER doors slid open and they rolled the gurney past her.

All of the commotion had upset Gracie. She stared wide-eyed around the room and burst into tears.

"It's okay, Grace. I promise mommy's going to be okay." The tremor in his voice rocked Olivia's world.

There was a chance Grace would never see her mother again, or him his wife. That fact pushed her forward.

"Mr. Bartholomew."

He looked at her. "Yes."

"Let me help. I'll take her. You need to be with your wife."

Gracie turned her damp baby brown gaze on Olivia and stopped crying.

"You know my wife?"

"I met her and Gracie this morning. I'm Olivia Morgan."

His hesitation evaporated. "Thank you. Judy's mom, Charlotte, is on her way now. She'll be here any minute." He handed Grace off and raced down the hall to the trauma room where the medical staff worked to save Judy Bartholomew's life.

Without conscious effort Olivia cuddled the baby and began to sway gently, rocking her in her arms in a timeless maternal rhythm.

The mechanical grind of the ER doors pulled her attention to the entrance as a man came inside holding his arm next to his body.

A nurse spotted him and moved forward at a brisk pace. "Mr. Dowdy. Come this way and we'll get your shoulder taken care of."

Olivia turned her back to the man, obscuring Gracie's view. She didn't need another stranger passing through her little world; as it was, her eyelids flicked open every time there was a loud sound.

"I took a header off my ATV. Good thing I was

wearing a helmet." The injured man's voice trailed off as he followed the nurse into an exam room somewhere down the hall.

Staring down at Grace, Olivia realized that the child was finally asleep, oblivious to the fight going on just down the hall.

Sadness flooded her heart. What would happen to Grace if Judy didn't survive? She'd seen how much they loved each other.

The automatic doors slid open and an older woman rushed into the ER, spotting the baby in Olivia's arms.

"Gracie." She reached out and touched the baby's cheek. "Where is she?" she asked, wiping at her eyes with the back of her hand.

"Down the hall, on the right. They're working on her."

"Thank you. I'll be right back to take her."

Olivia nodded, watching what she assumed was Judy's mother hurry down the hall to her daughter. Several moments later, she stepped out of the trauma room and moved toward them. From the pace of her steps, Olivia sensed the news wasn't good.

"Thank you for holding her."

"You're welcome. I just hope Judy pulls through." Reluctantly, she put Gracie into her grandmother's waiting arms and stepped back.

"She's so perfect."

Her grandma nodded, letting a brief smile tug at her mouth before she sobered. "Yes. Yes, she is."

Olivia turned around and left the ER through the double doors. Once they closed behind her, she paused for a moment to pin down the collage of feelings scattering through her. Sorrow, anger and curiosity. If she took anything away, it was the fact that no one ever really knew what was going on in another person's head. Still, she wondered why on earth Judy Bartholomew would want to kill herself and leave baby Gracie without a mother.

HE WATCHED FROM a safe distance, ruminating over the emotions bubbling inside of her, but it was her thoughts of Judy Bartholomew that registered the extent of what they were capable of. He'd seen Olivia converse with Judy on the street just before she was hit. Had they seen it, too? Taken their wrath out on her, thereby proving his summation that no one was safe if they helped Olivia uncover the truth?

She walked to her car and climbed in. He didn't plan to follow her this time, he already knew where she was headed.

Putting his car in Drive, he pulled out onto the side street. It wouldn't be long before she started to figure things out. He didn't like what he planned to do next, but it was the only thing that would keep her alive.

OLIVIA SETTLED IN the hard metal chair in the basement archives of the *Gazette* and thumbed through the dusty microfiche tray containing information from thirty-plus years ago. She was looking for the proverbial needle in a haystack, but she'd been able to find Jack Trayborne's birth announcement. It seemed that his parents, Caroline and Martin J. Trayborne II, had been trying to have children for some time and were over-joyed when Jack arrived. He appeared to be Black's Cove royalty, judging by the article's slant and he'd been born two months to the day before the Trayborne Foundation's annual fund-raiser masquerade ball.

Olivia let a sneeze go and sat back in her chair. Maybe that was her benchmark. If the masquerade ball happened on the same set Saturday every year, she could use it to track information on the family. She could string together Jack's life. Somehow, she doubted he attended the shindig before he could walk.

Flipping forward four years, she found the date and pulled the fiche.

Olivia stood up, stretched and turned to the reader. She put the film in the machine and pushed it in under the light.

A touching picture came into focus on the front page. Annual Ball Raises Three Million Dollars for Medical Research.

"What kind of research?" she wondered aloud as she slid the feed forward and stopped on a picture of a woman dancing at the ball holding her young son. She didn't have to read the caption to know who she was looking at. Jack, age four, and his mother.

She pulled the feed open and took out the fiche, turning back to the tray. He'd lived a charmed life. At four, she'd been dragged in and out of hospital after hospital by her parents as they fought to help her little brother Ross.

Suddenly, struck by that old feeling of guilt, she shook it off and slipped the microfilm back into its place. She'd take a one-year jump, just for the heck of it. After that, she'd have to focus her search on his adult life. Maybe she could find a gossip column so that at least she'd be up on the buzz.

She pulled the film for the following year, and returned to the viewer.

She'd been at it for a couple of hours now and her belly was starting to grumble, not to mention her desire for some fresh air.

Olivia put the microfiche in the machine and pushed it into the feed. The headline leaped out at her, as she adjusted the focus. Annual Ball to Honor Trayborne Family Loss.

Scanning the article under the caption, she felt her throat tighten.

With the tragic deaths of Martin and Caroline Trayborne, in December of last year, and the devastating injuries to their five-year-old son, Jack, the Trayborne Foundation has established a memorial fund in their honor. The proceeds from this year's masquerade ball will go to help other children with traumatic brain injuries.

She couldn't stop her hand from shaking as she retrieved the microfiche, put it back and dug frantically for the right story, calming only after she pulled it out of the tray and turned to the viewer. She put the microfiche in and slid it into the feed.

Tragic Car Crash Claims the Lives of Local
Couple, Leaves Their Young Son in a Coma.
Martin and Caroline Trayborne were killed late
Monday afternoon when their car slid off a
mountain road and rolled down an embankment.
Neither one was wearing a seat belt at the time.
They were pronounced dead at the scene. Their
four-year-old son, Jack, is listed in critical condition at Deaconess Memorial Hospital and
remains in a coma. He was riding in a car seat
at the time of the accident, which most likely
saved his life.

Olivia swallowed hard and sat back, digesting the information. Jack's life had been charmed until this
happened, but he'd obviously survived.

Advancing the microfilm reader, she scanned for
more information. Near the end of the film, she found
what she was looking for.

Jack Trayborne has been moved to Black's Cove
Clinic by his grandfather, Dr. Martin Trayborne.
The boy is still in a coma and Dr. Trayborne feels
his grandson will be better served in his private
clinic. Young Jack Trayborne has been unresponsive since the December 10 accident that killed his
parents, Martin and Caroline.

A surge of excitement washed over her as she moved
the feed back, searching for the date of the newspaper's

release. Her hand stilled as she stared at the date. Three months before her brother was admitted.

She swallowed, suddenly overwhelmed with questions. Questions she was compelled to get answers for. This information only added to that need.

Her brother, Ross, and Jack Trayborne both had traumatic brain injuries as children and they'd been patients at Black's Cove Clinic at the same time.

But what did it mean?

Chapter Five

Olivia tried to relax as she edged closer to the Trayborne estate, focusing on the leaves in vivid oranges and reds, as they scattered around her car. The drive into the estate was long and winding, but her approach with Jack would be straightforward.

She'd never been very good at playacting. It was a thinly coated lie that always made her feel uncomfortable, but she planned to play it cool. She was simply the curious sister of a patient who'd once been treated at the clinic.

From everything she'd learned about Jack Trayborne, he was a man who seemed to care about his fellow citizens. The Trayborne Foundation gave generously to worthy causes. He was gorgeous and benevolent…and untouchable?

A tinge of guilt colored her thoughts and for the first time, she found herself hoping that maybe, just maybe, he was everything he appeared to be. Then she wouldn't have to vet him along with the truth. Whatever that might be.

The road narrowed just past the turn into the clinic.

Olivia shuddered, remembering her last trip down that road. The fire had been ruled arson. She'd read it in the *Gazette* this morning and there was an investigation. She prayed the blaze had destroyed any evidence she'd ever been there. She was sure she'd left more than a few fingerprints and her lucky red ball cap. She pulled in a breath and tried to focus on the task at hand.

Slowing to a crawl, she came to a stop.

An ornate archway with a family crest and the name Trayborne forged in wrought iron marked the entrance to the estate.

She turned onto the lane lined with tall trees on both sides. A veil of mist hung in the air and seemed to emanate from everywhere and nowhere, deepening as she maneuvered her car along the drive.

Did everything out here have to exude creep? Too bad. She wouldn't turn back now. And even if she wanted to, she couldn't. Her investigation had ground to a stop. Talking to Jack was the only way, short of a court order, to get the facts. The grade steepened and leveled off just before the shadow of the mansion loomed in front of her.

For an instant, she doubted her approach and eased down on the brake. She turned chicken for a minute, something that had happened only a dozen times in her life. Returning her foot to the accelerator, she rolled through the gatehouse and pulled into the circle drive in front of the house.

It looked oddly like the clinic.

Glancing into the rearview mirror to pat her hair, she nearly jumped out of her skin.

He stood ten feet behind her car holding the reins of a big black horse.

Jack Trayborne. She knew his eyes. Swallowing, she gathered her nerve, climbed out of her car, shut the door and moved toward him.

"Can I help you?" he asked, staring at her with an intensity she could feel in her bones.

"Yes. I'm looking for Jack Trayborne."

"You're in luck." He stepped toward her, leading the magnificent horse with him. "I'm Jack Trayborne." He extended his hand. She reached out and took it. A rush of electricity jolted her and zinged up her arm. He squeezed with a firm grip and didn't immediately let go.

"But then, I'm sure you already knew that, Miss Morgan."

Tension coiled her nerves like a spring. She put on an apologetic smile and looked him in the eye. She'd been outed. "Then you know why I'm here?"

He held a blue gaze on her that made her ears burn. She returned it with one of her own. She wouldn't be intimidated by him. She wouldn't back down just because he made her nerves fray and her insides feel, well…bothered.

Sucking in courage with a deep breath of air, she leaned against the back of her car and prepared for battle.

"Nothing goes on in Black's Cove, Miss Morgan, that I'm not aware of."

"That's just creepy, Mr. Trayborne."

A slow touché sort of smile bowed his mouth and she

found her gaze locked on his lips. This odd attraction certainly wasn't intentional. Some other driving force was at work here. Hormones.

"Come with me. I've got to put Odin up. Then we'll talk."

That was encouraging, she thought, as he turned and led the horse away. She fell in step well back from the animal's rear hooves, hooves she was sure could take her head off with a single kick.

Fog swallowed horse and rider and only the rhythmic clop of hooves on cobblestone alerted her to the direction Jack and Odin had taken.

Olivia zipped up her sweatshirt and pulled on her hood to block out the dampness that permeated the air and soaked into her skin. It was only then that she realized the horse had stopped. Her compass was gone.

She stopped, too, listening for direction in the silent air around her.

A knot formed in her gut. The hair at her nape stood at attention. She was lost. About to turn back for her car, somewhere in the direction she'd just come, she felt a hand grasp her elbow.

She startled and jerked around, prepared to fight.

"Miss Morgan?"

Staring long and hard at Jack Trayborne, her fears calmed, soothed by his close proximity.

"I got lost for a minute."

"Black's Cove is a hundred yards in front of us. It produces evaporation fog, but it will lift soon."

He didn't release her, but it didn't bother her. The

contact sent a constant flow of heat through her and even though she found it unnerving, she wasn't going to break the contact so she could go stumbling off into the mist.

"How do you ride a horse in this pea soup?"

"Simple. I rely on my other senses…and Odin knows his way around. Between the two of us, we get to where we're going."

Great, another degree on the creep-o-meter.

From out of nowhere, a man stepped into their path.

Jack came to a stop and handed the reins to him, still grasping her arm.

"How was your ride, sir?"

"Uneventful, Stuart."

"That's what I like to hear." He turned, led the horse away and vanished in the fog as quickly as he'd appeared. Only the lingering clatter of hoof beats hedged her belief that he was an apparition rather than flesh and blood, and what the heck did "uneventful" mean? Maybe that Odin hadn't tossed him or stepped in a hole, the hazards of riding blind, she guessed.

"Don't let him spook you, Miss Morgan. Stuart's been tending the horses on the Trayborne estate since I climbed on my first pony. I can assure you he's very much alive."

"How did you know he freaked me out?"

"Because you're shaking." He turned toward her, releasing her elbow.

Olivia's breath hung in her throat. She stared up at Jack, taken with the searching way he looked at her. He was even more magnetic up close and she resisted the intense desire to lean into him.

"Can we talk now?"

His eyes narrowed for an instant. "Come inside," he said. "Take the chill off with something hot."

He grasped her elbow and guided her forward. "I trust your stay at my hotel has been satisfactory since the break-in?"

Caught off guard by the out-of-nowhere question, she fielded it and tried to relax. Of course he knew who she was. He'd responded to the break-in of her hotel room. A measure of relief spread through her body, leaving her almost giddy.

"No problems so far. Have there been other break-ins?"

"No. Yours is the first since I acquired the hotel five years ago."

"Well…Black's Cove seems to be a safe place to live." *If you didn't count half the time she'd been here.*

"Have the authorities recovered your laptop?"

"No." She doubted they ever would, but she hoped her story would fair much better than her stolen computer. She'd already recompiled the beginning; now she needed the middle.

"Here we are." He led her up the steps to the house and opened the massive front door.

Olivia stepped through the entrance into the foyer with Jack behind her. She was struck by the lavishly appointed entry. Charmed. Jack lived a charmed life, but he'd been through a lot in his early years. A moment of hesitation held up her need to question him, but she diluted it with the knowledge that he was the only one with the answers about the clinic and what they'd done to Ross.

She pushed her hood back and turned toward him. "I'm not here to hash out the break-in at your hotel. I'm here to speak to you about Black's Cove Clinic."

He froze in mid-task, but continued removing his jacket in a decidedly stiff fashion. "The clinic is closed, Miss Morgan. Has been for many years."

"I know. The information I want dates back thirty years and has to do with your grandfather's research into traumatic brain injuries in children."

If he was at all rattled by her request, it didn't manifest itself in his hard-set features.

"And what is your interest in the data, Miss Morgan, other than the interesting fact that you sell to an exposé rag, bent on printing wild fabrications that destroy honest medical professionals' lives and careers?"

A defensive response bubbled up her throat, but she held her tongue. He wanted her to explode, to end the conversation in a barrage of threats, but she didn't plan to take the bait. Getting a court order for the medical records would be almost impossible and a fight like that could leave her impoverished, while Jack Trayborne barely touched his vast fortune.

"My exposé deals only in facts, Mr. Trayborne. In the last five years, I've uncovered seven cases of medical mistakes that have caused trauma and death. Putting them under the microscope helps the public make better, more informed choices."

"I doubt you've come here to discuss the ramifications of stories like those that only work to drive up the cost of malpractice insurance and ultimately the price of health care across the board. So let's get to the specifics of what you really want, Miss Morgan."

Olivia scrambled for words in the heat of the moment, but she was caught up in the argument he'd laid out, an argument she'd pondered herself more than once.

"My brother Ross was treated at the clinic more than thirty years ago. I want access to his medical records and an explanation for why the Trayborne Foundation set up a trust fund for him. I want to know if it was penance for a medical mistake."

A muscle jumped along Jack's jawline, now as rigid as tempered steel. She'd hit a nerve and with a couple more strategic digs, she might get some answers. "Look, he's the only family I have left. My parents are dead and Ross is my responsibility now. I need to know what happened to him."

For an instant, he softened, his gaze locking with hers and she felt pinned in place, X-rayed by the intense way he looked at her.

"The clinic's medical records are privileged. The moment your parents signed the papers locking in the trust, your brother's file was sealed. There's a confidentiality clause."

Anger sizzled through her, leaving her on fire. "He's my flesh and blood. I have a right to know what your grandfather did to him in the clinic. I have a right to know if it contributed to his current condition."

"And if you find out my grandfather tried to save something that was unsavable and there was no wrong-doing, what then?"

She stared at him, searching for words. She'd never had that problem. Not even once. "Well, I suppose I'd have to…." What would she do? Print the truth?

"There you have it, Miss Morgan. Which is why I won't expose the clinic or its medical records to libel. If you insist on pursuing it, you'll have to get a court order to unseal your brother's medical file."

Olivia rocked back on her heels, caught off balance as he moved toward her. She had no recourse; he was right. She took a step back. "You were there along with my brother."

He paused, never taking his gaze off her, but where she expected to see hostility, she saw an instance of pain cross his features before he looked away.

"Yes. I was in the clinic at the same time as your brother Ross, but I was five, Miss Morgan. Hardly old enough to tie my own shoes, much less remember him."

A knot squeezed her throat shut. She swallowed hard. Could she continue to drive the conversation forward? It made her feel like an out-of-control papa-razzo stalking a celebrity, unwilling to back off for fear of missing that one perfect shot.

"I'm sorry, but I can't let this go. I need to know what happened to him. And I don't plan to stop until I have the answers. If it takes a court order, Mr. Trayborne, then I'll find a way to get one."

She turned toward the door, but he was on her before she had time to react. He grasped her upper arms and held her firmly in place.

A jolt of heat streaked through her body and left her tingling all over. She was drawn to him. She stared up into his face, mesmerized by the glimmer in his eyes as he stared at her. She was helpless to resist the wave of energy that rooted her to the spot like a tractor beam.

"You have to stop, Olivia. You're in danger as long as you stay in Black's Cove. Go home. Let this go."

A measure of agreement coiled around her thoughts. She'd almost been annihilated twice. Would a third time be the charm? Caution stirred in her blood. How did he know she was in danger…unless he was behind it?

Unlinking the invisible chain that held them together, she stepped back, her body missing the contact with a primal need she couldn't put a name to. She reached for the door knob and turned it.

"If you're threatening me, it's not going to work. I came to Black's Cove for a story and I'm not leaving without one."

"Better no story than dead."

His words echoed in her brain as she jerked open the door, bent on digging so deep into Jack's past that she'd end up in proverbial China.

Tendrils of mist reached out and swallowed her the moment she stepped outside. She aimed for her car and escape, determined to expose Jack Trayborne no matter what it took, including a court order.

He heightened his senses, picking up a low voltage hum that mixed and separated with the beat of Olivia's footsteps against the cobblestone drive outside, it's source emanating from somewhere underneath her car.

Alarm forced him into action. He threw open the door, spotting her less than twenty feet away and about to round the driver's side fender of the death trap.

Reaching out, he focused his energies and lifted her off her feet, dragging her to him like a rag doll at the end of a rubber band.

They collided just as the bomb detonated.

Desperate to save her, Jack pulled her into his arms and dived inside the door a fraction of a second before the percussion wave.

Together, they slammed to the marble floor. He covered her body with his.

The glass panels flanking the entrance imploded.

Molten glass blew into the foyer, its shards raining down like a hail of bullets around them.

Listening for the sound of her heartbeat, he was satisfied to hear it drumming in even time beneath him. He raised up and glanced out to where her car sat in the drive, a mass of burning rubble.

She'd been seconds from death, but how had they gotten past his senses this morning and planted a bomb in her car? He'd warned them to leave her alone. He heightened his senses, searching for answers in the chaos, but he came up empty.

Reaching down, he rolled her over in his arms. Her

head lulled to the side, sending a rush of worry through him. She'd been knocked out in the blast.

The clop of hurried footsteps coming across the foyer pulled his attention to Frances, his housekeeper.

"I heard an explosion! Are you okay, sir?"

"Yes." Jack came to his knees and pulled Olivia into his arms. "Can you please get me my first aid kit? Miss Morgan needs to be cleaned up."

Frances hurried away and Jack carried Olivia into the front parlor under the stairs, where he laid her down on the sofa.

The flying glass had managed to leave her face riddled with small cuts.

Frances rushed into the room, carrying his medical kit.

"Shall I call the police?" she asked as she undid the kit's zipper and placed the open kit on the coffee table in front of him.

"No, not yet, but ask Stuart to get some water on the fire before it spreads."

"Yes, sir." Frances left the room in a hurry and he listened to her footsteps fade into the distance.

Pulling a sterile pad from his kit, he opened a small bottle of antiseptic and moistened the gauze. He dabbed at the blood coating a series of cuts across the right side of her face, examining them for glass in the process. They were clean.

He took an ammonia capsule from his kit, popped it open and waved it under Olivia's nose.

Her response was rapid. She bolted upright, nearly

knocking him off the sofa. Wide-eyed and agitated, she glared at him.

"How do you feel?"

Olivia reached up and patted the side of her head, pulling back fingertips spotted with blood. The last thing she remembered was rushing toward Jack and hearing an ear-splitting explosion.

"What happened?"

"Your car blew up in the driveway."

She stared at him, grasping at the implications of what he'd just said. Someone had tried to kill her again?

"Call the police. This makes the third time in a week."

"The third time? You mean this has happened before?"

When would she learn to keep her mouth zipped? "I was almost killed on Main Street this morning by a runaway car, but I'm sure you already know that. I saw you in the crowd."

A twinkle of amusement glinted in his intense blue eyes. Her breath caught in her throat. He was so damn sexy…and close, she couldn't find spit to swallow.

"And when was the first time, Olivia?"

He was treading too close to the truth. There wasn't a chance she'd tell him close call *numero uno* had come in the basement of Black's Cove Clinic. That admission could be accompanied by a charge of breaking and entering.

Tension twisted around her nerve endings. "It doesn't matter. I need to get out of here and you need to call the police or the bomb squad."

"If you want me to call the authorities, I will."

Why did she get the feeling that would only bring about more trouble? And why did she suddenly feel safer here, with him, than she'd ever felt in her life?

Chapter Six

Olivia crossed her arms against the penetration of the late-afternoon fog through her clothing. The mist had remained locked in all afternoon and now added a spooky aura around the burned-out scrap of smoldering metal that had once been her car.

"Do you have any idea who would want to hurt you, Miss Morgan?"

She glanced at the officer in front of her and shook her head, allowing her gaze to slide back to the rubble visible just over his left shoulder.

"We're ready to wrap things up for the night. If you think of anything, will you call me?" He handed her a business card and she shoved it in the back pocket of her jeans.

"I will. Hey, can I catch a ride back into town?"

The officer paused. "Jack said he'd drive you to your hotel."

The feel of a hand pressed against the small of her back, ignited her senses. There was little she could do to stop the officer as he turned and retreated back to the investigation taking place just in front of her.

They'd found the source of the explosion, or rather, what was left of it. A smattering of twisted bomb parts.

Olivia swallowed and responded to the increasing pressure against her skin.

"Come back inside." The coaxing note in Jack's voice seemed to sooth her frazzled nerves and she tried to relax, letting him turn her back into the house.

"Muriel, my chef, has prepared dinner. Join me first, then I'll drive you back to the hotel."

Her first mental response, a resounding *no,* seemed rude and inhospitable. Besides, she was starving and physically exhausted. What could it hurt to sit across the table from her nemesis for an hour? She owed him her life. If he hadn't saved her, she'd be in pieces, just like her poor car.

"I'll stay," she needed to quantify the acceptance, "for an hour."

"An hour it is, then." He grasped her hand and pulled it through the crook of his arm.

The contact sent a tremor through her followed by a rush of heat, and she was suddenly aware of how she must look, covered in residue from the blast, holes burned in the sleeve of her shirt, and her hair… Olivia's footsteps slowed. She pulled free of her and Jack's formal attachment. This wasn't a date to the prom.

"Maybe you should take me home now."

He stopped and turned to her. Reaching out, he lifted her chin with his hand, lining up their gazes.

Her breath hung up in her lungs and for a moment, she allowed her reservations to slip as she stared at his lips.

"For someone quite literally blown into my arms, you look pretty good." A slow seductive smile pulled up the corners of his mouth and her traitorous knees threatened to wobble out from underneath her. Was he a mind reader? Or just an experienced playboy who knew the heart of a woman and her desire to look her best whenever she engaged with the opposite sex? She chose the latter.

"So you're not worried I'll wreck your furniture?"

His eyes sparked with amusement. "I'm more concerned that you won't. That you'll leave here and whoever wants you dead will try again, and I won't be there to catch you."

Olivia sobered. "I've been taking care of myself for a long time. I don't need to be caught."

He grasped her hand, pulled it through the crook of his arm again and led her deeper into the house. "And what of your family, Olivia? Did they not take care of you?"

How on God's green earth had this conversation digressed into a discussion about her family's care or lack thereof?

"Sir?" An older woman in a pristine white apron stepped into their path near the archway of a massive dining room. "Do you have a wine request this evening?"

"Yes. Have Stuart go to the cellar and retrieve a special bottle from my private reserve. White bordeaux, 1937."

The woman's face constricted for a moment before she nodded and turned away, disappearing down the hall and presumably to alert spooky Stuart the horseman of his required task.

"My family cared deeply for me, Jack." The retort was crisp and intended to end the uncomfortable conversation, but it didn't work.

"It must have been difficult for you…having them consumed with concern for Ross?"

His observation twisted her muscles into knots. "I survived and so did they."

He led her to the end of a long table where two place settings had been laid out. Releasing her, he pulled out her chair and pushed it back in once she'd seated herself.

"Thank you," she whispered, wondering if she'd died and been launched back a hundred years? Not only was Jack Trayborne gorgeous, but he was a gentleman, too.

Jack took his seat. "The Trayborne Foundation likes to know that our efforts have helped families with severely injured children. Not only the children themselves, but every member of the immediate family as well."

She smiled, covering up the tangle of emotions she could feel squeezing the life out of her. "Your work is beneficial. A toast, then?" She reached out and picked up the crystal water goblet in front of her plate.

Jack followed suit.

"To the Trayborne Foundation, providers of goodness and light." The ting of the glasses coming together relieved some of the tension that wrapped her body. She just wanted this conversation to end.

She took a cursory sip from her water glass and set it back down in front of her, determined to change the subject.

"So, tell me about the Phantom of Black's Cove."

Jack slowly put down his glass, feeling the first sensations of anticipation start to stir in his blood. "You've heard the talk around town?"

"I saw a story in the *Gazette* the other day, about an elderly couple who survived a car accident. They claim they were saved by the Phantom. There were whispers of my having his protection after I was hit by the car. Maybe there's something to it."

He kept his face placid as he watched her.

"You've lived in Black's Cove your entire life, surely you've heard of him?"

Caution hedged Jack's words and laced around his response. "Yes. I've heard of him."

"Ah, but do you believe in him?"

"I think it's rooted in the human psyche to believe in things you cannot see. It's called faith. Does that make him real? I don't know."

He liked the way her cheeks pinked under his scrutiny, the way she'd avoided answering his questions about her family, but he resisted the need to reach into her mind, to find out what she was hiding and why it made her so uncomfortable.

The swinging door leading from the kitchen opened, and Muriel bustled through carrying two plates of food. Stuart was right behind her with the requested bottle of wine.

They sat in silence until the food was served, the wine poured and the staff gone.

Reaching out, Jack picked up his wineglass and raised it in a toast. "To the Phantom for saving your life."

Olivia raised her glass, too, and took a long swallow after the salute. "When did this stuff start showing up in the newspaper?"

"Years ago. A county paint crew was doing high work on a bridge over the river, when one of the workers fell and his safety line snapped. He was miraculously stopped from hitting the water three-hundred feet below. Eyewitnesses said he hovered a foot above the water for a moment before dropping unharmed into it, where he was rescued by a fisherman in a passing motor boat."

Olivia raised her eyebrows and let out a breath. "I'm sure there's a reasonable explanation." She picked up her fork and knife and cut into the meat on her plate. "Maybe he broke his fall by spreading out his body… like a wind brake."

"Maybe." Jack studied her face, watching her chew as she worked the problem in her mind. "Anything is possible."

"Mmm, this is wonderful. What is it?"

"Kobe beef."

She sliced off another piece, her motor skills beginning to show signs of discord. A physical reaction to the sedative lacing her water and activated by the wine.

Separately, they were harmless; intertwined, they would keep her sedated until morning.

He hated the method he'd been forced to use to keep her here tonight. She wasn't safe and until he could stop them from trying to kill her again, he would employ whatever tactic worked.

"I'm so…tired," she said, staring at him with a relaxed smile on her full lips. Wisps of tangled blond hair framed her dirt-smudged face. Her sleepy, eyelids-half-closed gaze about drove him over the edge and churned a measurable degree of desire in his blood. She was as beautiful and seductive as she was persistent and as much as he wanted to touch her, he knew he couldn't risk it.

He reached out at the precise moment her head drooped forward and caught her before she went face first into her dinner plate.

Stuart stepped out of the shadows next to the doorway and moved to his side. "Can I assist you, sir?"

"Dump the wine and her water, leave the bottle and glasses on the table, then ask Frances to prepare the suite next to mine. Miss Morgan has had too much to drink, she'll be spending the night."

Jack gently leaned Olivia back in her chair, stood up and pulled her into his arms. He'd deal with her questions in the morning, of that he was sure, but for tonight, she would be safe.

JACK PAUSED in the darkness next to Rick Dowdy's sleeping figure, long enough to cool his anger. He was certain Rick had planted this afternoon's car bomb with the intention of killing Olivia. The only question was why Dowdy had chosen to ignore his warning.

Reaching out, he caught the sleeping man by the throat in an invisible stranglehold, and raised him up into a sitting position before dropping him and surrounding him in an energy field.

Dowdy coughed and sucked in a ragged breath, coming fully awake.

"Dammit, Jack, what are you trying to do, kill me?" He reached for his neck, covering it with his free hand. His other arm hung in a sling, a casualty of their encounter in the warehouse. Rick trained a leery stare on him as he regained his composure.

"Where were you this afternoon?"

"What are you, my mother?"

He stepped closer, prepared to squeeze an answer out of Rick if necessary.

Rick's eyes widened. "Back off…hold on. I was slamming back brewskies at McCreary's Pub. I was there at noon. They put me in a cab at nine. I've been here ever since, sleeping it off. You can ask the bartender. He'll back me up."

Jack heightened his senses, pulling in a lungful of air, picking up the stench of alcohol emanating from Dowdy's blood stream.

He had serious doubts the man possessed the wits to construct a bomb. The only thing he'd ever done with his trust money was take it in liquid form, but he reached for his thoughts anyway.

What he pulled back satisfied him that he had no involvement in the afternoon's attack.

"Make sure you continue to steer clear of Miss Morgan."

Rick's eyes narrowed. "She'll take us all down, Jack."

Taking a step back, he turned and left the room. Diana was next; he had to rule her out, as well.

He left Rick's place and covered the three blocks to her house, in a hurry, past the neighbor's barking dog, where he reached out and closed the dog's mouth until he'd moved past.

Stopping in the alley, he heightened his senses, scanning the entire area. It was clear.

Jack opened the back gate and strode up the sidewalk, taking the steps up to the door in stealth mode.

He raised his fist to knock, but the door opened before he could rap on it.

Diana Moore stood just inside, tying the belt of her robe. "Jack, what are you doing here?"

"Are you alone?"

"Yeah, but I wouldn't be if you'd come inside." A seductive smile pulled her thin lips apart and he found himself making a comparison with Olivia's full luscious ones.

It bothered him.

"Where were you this afternoon?"

"Where I always am, the pet shop. I've got an order going out in the morning to the lab in Atlanta. I was filling it."

"Good. Stay out of trouble, Diana. Good night." He stepped back and moved off the porch, hearing the door click shut. There was a time when he would have stayed with her, a time when he did. She understood the pitfalls of his existence, understood he could never open his heart to her or anyone else.

He walked down the sidewalk, through the gate and into the alley, muzzling the dog once again as he passed the Chamberlains' home. Taking a left, he hurried down the street to his car and climbed in. He needed to get back to Olivia. Her drug-induced slumber would subside at dawn.

OLIVIA STOOD IN the doorway of the dining room the next morning staring at the empty wine bottle and the two goblets next to it. She didn't remember much after her first glass, but they must have drained the entire bottle together.

Glancing around, she tried to relax her bunched nerves. The cavernorus place was quiet. She moved to the table, picked up the bottle and held it to her nose. Taking a whiff, she tried to detect anything out of the ordinary. She was no wine connoisseur, but bouquet wasn't what she was smelling for. How was it possible she'd consumed enough alcohol to wind up in one of Jack Trayborne's beds for the night?

"Did you enjoy it, Olivia? I've got another bottle in the cellar."

Startled, she banged the bottle down on the table and whirled around.

Jack stood in the entryway, arms crossed over his bare chest. A pair of navy blue silk pajama bottoms hung low on his narrow hips and a stray piece of dark hair splayed against his forehead. He was the best-looking bed head she'd ever seen.

She swallowed hard and worked to maintain eye contact, feeling embarrassment flash hot on her cheeks. "Yes. It was very good. 1937, what a great year for white bordeaux."

A smile parted his lips and he stepped toward her. "I didn't believe you were in any condition to leave here last night. I trust you slept well?"

"Yes, I did."

Muriel pushed through the door from the kitchen carrying a newspaper and a cup of coffee. "Sir." She handed the items off to Jack.

"Thank you. Perhaps Miss Morgan would like a cup?"

He trained his attention on her.

"No, thanks. My cab will be here any minute."

His jaw tensed, his eyes narrowing as he studied her. "You don't need a cab. I'd be happy to take you back to the hotel."

The sensation of being held in place overwhelmed her senses and she took a step forward just to prove she could. "You've been a generous host, Jack, but I have to get back to work digging around in your past. That is, unless you want to tell me about the clinic and NPQ?"

His eyes darkened from medium blue to light sapphire. He had to know what NPQ was. What else did he know?

"I didn't think so." She stepped past him, seeing for the first time the fine etching of scar tissue crisscrossing his torso like a road map. Remnants of his past received in the accident that killed his parents?

"I'll let myself out."

He turned and she felt his contemplative gaze on her backside. It wasn't a totally unpleasant experience, but that fact bothered her and the residual sensation stayed with her even after she climbed in the waiting taxi for the ride back to town.

JACK READ THROUGH Ross Morgan's medical file once more before he put it down and rocked back in his chair.

Out of the original Black's Cove seven test group, Ross was the only patient who hadn't responded to the NPQ formula. His grandfather had never been able to determine why. But could he give Olivia the information, without risking full exposure of the entire group, himself included?

Maybe he could black out the other test subjects' names and their results. It could work, but she was smart. Smart enough to figure out what those results produced? If so, she would expose them all.

Jack closed his eyes, searching for a solution, but in his gut, he knew she wasn't going to stop asking questions until she got answers. Answers that could get her killed.

Frustrated, he opened his eyes and stood up, feeling the fringe of euphoria that always preceded a precognitive vision. He slumped against the edge of his desk in a waking dream.

Who would it be this time? Whose life would hang in

the balance waiting for his intervention? Which citizen of Black's Cove would he rescue in the nick of time?

OLIVIA STARED at the number coming up on her cell phone screen, a number she didn't recognize.

Flipping it open, she answered. "Hello?"

"Miss Morgan?" A female voice whispered over the connection.

"Yes. Who's this?"

"Just listen."

Caution ignited in her brain and she contemplated closing the phone on the mystery caller.

"I have information about Jack Trayborne and what went on at Black's Cove Clinic. Are you interested?"

Excitement surged in her veins, but it was quickly diluted by an ounce of reality. Nothing was free.

"What's it going to cost me?"

The line went silent and she almost shook the phone to get the woman talking again.

"Nothing."

She hesitated to respond, a measure of suspicion holding her in check. "I don't believe you."

"Jack Trayborne has secrets, Miss Morgan."

"How did you get this number?" Her mind stuck on the detail. She'd only given out her cell number to the hotel and the cops, no one else, but it was listed in her missing laptop. Could that be the source? Was she speaking with the woman who'd stolen it?

"Be at the roadside park on Highway 21 at twelve sharp today. I'll leave an envelope taped to the bottom of the picnic table in area number one. If you like that sample, you can have more. Just call the number on the note and I'll be there."

"I don't believe—" The line went dead. She pulled the phone away from her ear, hit redial and listened to the call go through.

After seven rings, she was about to give up.

"Hello?" A male voice answered.

"Who is this?"

"Dean."

"Where have I called?"

"A pay phone on 10th street in Black's Cove."

"Sorry." Olivia hung up and sat down on the bed. What to do? There had to be someone besides Jack who knew what went on at the clinic thirty years ago. But could she trust an anonymous caller on a pay phone, who just happened to know her cell number?

No...no...no. But she was fresh out of leads. She knew the park in question. A restroom, three or four picnic spots, on the main highway...in broad daylight.

Glancing at her watch, she stood up, grabbed her purse and the keys to the car she'd rented this morning.

She had ten minutes to get to the roadside park six miles away.

JACK FLOORED THE Jaguar and whipped around a red Pontiac creeping along in front of him.

The details of the precognitive vision were burned in his brain and repeated in a cyclic stream that made his heart hammer and his hands sweat.

He should never have let her leave this morning and if he managed to get to her in time, he didn't plan on letting her go again.

OLIVIA FASTENED HER seat belt and slipped the key into the ignition. The compact fired up and she rolled out of the hotel parking lot headed for the back way out of town.

Mentally, she ran over her checklist, satisfied she'd brought along everything she needed, including a tape recorder just in case the information was substantial and she decided to take the mystery caller up on her offer for more.

Traffic was light to nonexistent as she reached the edge of town where the speed limit increased and everything opened up into the countryside.

Olivia pressed down on the accelerator.

The car sputtered, surged forward, sputtered again and stalled.

"Shoot!" She stepped on the brake, rolled to a stop and put the car in Park. Glancing in the rearview mirror, she made sure there was no one there to rear-end her before she got the engine started again.

She turned the key.

The engine fired. The car roared back to life. Olivia gunned the motor, put the car in gear and took off again, checking the clock on the dashboard—11:53.

She was going to be late.

Worry frayed her nerves. Would the information disappear if she didn't show up on time? Reacting to the thought, she pressed down on the accelerator. The car picked up speed, the speedometer needle climbing to fifty in a forty-five zone.

Olivia let off the gas, but the needle moved steadily higher.

Panic clamped on her nerves. She put her foot on the brake.

Fifty-five…

Up ahead in the distance, she saw the blinking red warning lights of a railroad crossing come on.

The letters of an acronym AOT, always on time, zipped by in her brain. The 11:55 freight was always on time.

She stomped on the brake pedal.

A puff of smoke rolled out behind the car as the tires grabbed the pavement. The car didn't slow.

Sixty…

Olivia reached up and jerked the gear shift into neutral, the engine revved, the car moved faster.

Sixty-five…

She forced the shift lever into Park.

Gears ground. The transmission locked up, disintegrating from underneath the vehicle, but it didn't stop.

Seventy…

On her right and closing in fast she saw the train, heard its shrill whistle above the racket coming from the possessed car.

Jump! She had to jump.

Olivia grabbed for her seat belt closure and pressed the release button. It didn't open.

With all the strength she had, she pulled the steering wheel to the left, but the car didn't respond. It continued on a collision course.

A destiny with a freight train.

Chapter Seven

Jack slammed on the brakes, locking them up as he rounded the corner just ahead of the locomotive, and jumped out of the car.

He channeled his energy, focusing it on the freight train roaring down the tracks. If he cast it on her car, it would be torn apart with her inside. He didn't doubt that someone was controlling her vehicle and twin energy fields always caused an explosion.

Reaching out, he felt the sixty-ton engine vibrate the ground under his feet. Its rumble was deafening, its momentum deadly.

"Stop!" he yelled, raising both his hands in a push-back position against the thundering wall of iron.

Sweat squeezed out of his pores as he strained to slow the train long enough for her to cross the tracks in front of it.

The screech of steel wheels on steel tracks split the air.

The noise coming from the train's diesel engines went up an octave, as the force he exerted on the locomotive over-revved its drive train and spun the wheels on the tracks.

A second longer…he could hold it back a second longer.

Olivia's car hit the tracks and shot past him.

He let go.

Half a second later, the train blasted by.

Turning around, Jack reached his palm out and took possession of the car. It rolled to a stop a hundred feet up the highway.

He ran for it.

Smoke belched from under the hood. The tires had been flattened by her attempts to stop the runaway vehicle with the brakes.

Anger surged in his veins. He'd told them to leave her alone. Warned them what would happen if they tried to hurt her again. This time, he'd make sure they stopped.

The driver's door opened. Olivia staggered out and collapsed in a heap next to the smoldering compact.

Reaching back, she repeatedly slugged her fist against the rear door of the car.

"Stupid! Stupid…car. Why didn't you stop?"

Jack slowed his pace, amused by her act of retaliation, but she had to be in shock. She'd missed being crushed by the train by less than half a second.

"Olivia?" He knelt on the ground next to her and raised her chin with his hand.

Her eyes went wide, like a frightened animal, desperate and confused. He pulled her into his arms. Her body trembled against his.

"It's okay. You're safe now."

She melted into him.

Reaching out, he stroked her silky hair with his hand. The contact sent desire, hot and urgent, rushing through him like a river, sweeping his resistance away in its relentless current.

He could hold back a train, but he could no longer hold back the need that had taken over his body, one cell at a time since the moment he'd seen her in a vision.

Olivia listened to the pounding of Jack's heart against her ear. Not even the click-clack of boxcar wheels on the track could drown it out. She breathed him in, feeling truly safe. The terror that had shattered her mind and heart only moments ago evaporated.

Pushing back from him, she stared up into his face. His eyes narrowed and she sensed his intent well before he leaned forward, aiming for her lips.

She closed her eyes an instant before contact. Anticipation stirred in her blood stream and trapped air in her lungs.

The kiss was sweet, shifting and changing as she put her arms around his neck. The intensity level shot up, taking her desire with it in boundless leaps that threatened to yank her restraint.

Jack retreated first, feeling the sensation of fire scorch his lips where he'd touched her. All reason had gone on hiatus the instant he took her mouth.

Rocking back, he stared at her. She'd been as dazed and consumed as he had been, but he resisted the need to reach for her thoughts and even though the train had passed, he felt like he'd been hit by it.

A timid smile spread on her mouth and threatened to pull him right back into the measure of heaven he'd just escaped.

"You're him." Her smile broadened. "You're the Phantom of Black's Cove. You saved me from being annihilated by that freight train."

Jack sobered. "No one knows who the Phantom is, Olivia. That's why he works."

"Then how in the heck do you explain what just happened?"

Tension knotted the muscles between his shoulder blades. "The accelerator on the car stuck wide open. The engineer saw you and was able to slow the train just enough that he narrowly missed crushing you."

Her gotcha look of glee vanished. "I wanted to believe."

"I know you did. Now why don't you tell me what you're doing out here?"

Olivia opened her mouth to speak, but thought better of it. Part of her wanted to tell him what had put her in the train's path. The other part knew she'd have to admit the phone conversation, but he was her ride to the park, and the information she so desperately needed.

"You know the roadside park on Highway 21?"

"Yes."

"I was headed there." She attempted to stand, using the side of the car to pull herself up onto her wobbly legs.

Jack reached out to steady her. Heat entered at the

site and radiated into her where they made contact. The desire to kiss him again raced across her mind.

"You know my life flashed before my eyes just before I crossed the tracks?"

"Really?"

"Yeah. I decided I haven't done enough kissing in my lifetime."

A sultry smile parted his lips and she returned one of her own.

He released her. "Changing the subject isn't going to work, Olivia, and as much as I enjoyed that kiss, you're still going to tell me what you're doing out here."

He was a mind reader judging by the amused look on his face.

"I got a call half an hour ago from a woman claiming to have information about Black's Cove Clinic…and… you."

His amusement was replaced by a look of concern. "And you bought it? Can't you see this was a ploy to put you smack in front of the 11:55?"

A chill skittered through her body. She hadn't considered that angle. "There's only one way to find out if she was telling the truth."

"And what's that?"

"Take me to the roadside park where the information is supposed to be hidden."

He crossed his arms over his broad chest and studied her, a tactic that made her squirm. If the information was where the caller said it would be, she could use it to expose his secrets. Find out what made him tick behind all those muscles and devastating good looks.

A quirky smile flashed on his mouth, but vanished before she could get a read on its source.

She reached inside the compact, grabbed her purse and pulled the strap over her shoulder.

"After you." He reached for her elbow and escorted her toward his car. "We'll call a tow truck, but I doubt there's much help for that car. I hope you took the supplemental insurance policy."

"Your humor sucks, Jack."

He laughed, a deep pleasant sound that infiltrated her mind and remained there long after they reached the low black Jag. She pulled in a deep breath as he opened the door and slid into the passenger seat, feeling drained.

She'd beaten death by a half second. It wasn't something she ever wanted to do again.

Jack hesitated next to the car, surveying the surrounding area for their hiding place. They had to be nearby. Heightening his senses, he combed the area for movement. Nothing.

He climbed in the car and made a U-turn. "You said a woman called you?"

"Yeah."

"Did she give you her name?"

"No."

His nerves tightened. Was it possible Diana lured Olivia onto the tracks? Everyone in town knew the 11:55 was always on time.

"Promise me if you get any more calls, you'll contact me…that you won't chase secrets alone." He glanced over at her, struck by the contemplative look on her face.

"My life really did flash in front of me the instant I realized I couldn't stop the car."

"You should consider yourself lucky. Most of us never get the motivation to change course."

"Who said I was going to change course? I'm just going to avoid those train tracks in the future."

She looked over at him, smiled and raised her eyebrows.

He instantly wanted to touch her, to absorb some of her optimism, but he held back. She had no idea what she was dealing with. What they were capable of. Hell, he was just beginning to realize it himself. They'd go to any length to keep their secret.

"Here it is." He slowed the car and turned into the park's empty parking lot. Easing to a stop, he tried to reconcile the blade of caution sawing back and forth over his nerves.

There was no one around, save the fall leaves that covered the grass and scattered in the wind. The door to the restroom stood open, a slave to the breeze rocking it back and forth.

"Where is this information supposed to be?"

"Taped to the bottom of the table in picnic area number one."

His gaze settled on a table to the left, situated under a large pine tree. "I'll go. You stay in the car. I don't like this."

"Cars don't like me. I'm not staying. I'm going with

you." Before he could stop her, she opened the door and climbed out.

He followed, his senses heightened the moment his feet hit the pavement. Something wasn't right. He combed the woods with his gaze, looking for movement.

"Let's hurry." He grasped Olivia's arm, steering her to the picnic table and standing guard as she knelt next to it and ran her hand along the edge.

"Nothing." She plopped down on the bench. "I've been duped, suckered, conned."

On the hillside above the park, Jack saw a flash of movement in his peripheral vision. The echo of a rifle shot blasted terror straight through him.

He lunged for Olivia, casting a shield around them at the same instant he pulled her to the ground. But he hadn't deployed soon enough.

Another shot cracked through the air, its bullet impacting the invisible wall protecting them.

Olivia rolled over, staring at the blue sky overhead. What was happening? She watched a slug slam into a watery bubble floating just above her face. It stopped cold and tumbled onto the ground next to her. "What is this?" She poked at it.

"It's an energy field, but we have to get out of here. I've been hit."

Terror shook her. She rolled over and saw the sleeve of Jack's shirt. Crimson and spreading fast.

"I'll protect us, but we have to get to the car."

Olivia worked to wrap her mind around what was happening. *Think…think…think.*

She yanked her blouse out of the waistband of her jeans and ripped the bottom off it. Wrapping the material several times around Jack's upper arm, she pulled it tight to stem the bleeding.

Helping him to his feet, she flinched as another slug splayed on the bubble.

It didn't matter that she must be going nuts. It didn't matter that things like this only happened in science fiction movies. It didn't matter that it didn't matter. She had to save Jack. But an explanation would be something she demanded after they survived.

"Stay close. I can only shield us together in a three-foot area."

Reaching out he took her hand. The contact had a magnetic quality that made her heart race. They broke into a jog.

Four more shots bounced off the field before they reached the car.

Jack pulled open the driver's door. She slid in first, he followed. He fired the engine, backed up and floored the gas pedal. The car rocketed forward. Jack barely braked before he pulled out onto the highway.

Olivia didn't breathe normally again until they were racing away from the park.

"Wait. Where are you going?"

"Home."

Panic shook her nerves. "You need medical attention. We need to turn around and go to the hospital."

"They're required to file a report with the police department if a gun shot wound comes in. There will be lots of questions, Olivia. Questions I'd rather not answer. It's a flesh wound. The bullet went through and through. We can take care of it at home."

He was right. Of course he was right. They'd ask her what happened and she'd tell them how her car had taken over and attempted to ram her into a moving freight train, how an invisible bubble had stopped a barrage of bullets meant to blast them full of holes...

"They'd cart me off to the nut house."

"My point exactly."

She tried to put it all together. There was that Phantom thing again. The same phenomenon had protected her from the car on Main Street, she was sure of it, felt it in her heart, and no matter how many times Jack denied it, she was sure he was the Phantom, lifesaver of Black's Cove. But he needed anonymity. She'd give it to him for now. But how had he known where she'd be?

"How'd you find me?"

He cast her a sideways glance that sent her heart rate up. "I was worried about you this morning after you left. I decided to come into town to check on you."

She could see right through him. Besides, how did he know she'd be in that car? If he was the Phantom, he'd have saved whoever was behind the wheel. Her bravado deflated.

Jack slowed the Jaguar and made the turn into the estate. His arm throbbed. How was Olivia going to react to the lab where his grandfather had worked out the details of NPQ? He was going to have to placate her somehow.

He'd blacked out everything in Ross's file that could possibly spark her need to know. Would it be enough? Somehow he doubted it. Olivia Morgan was on a quest for something more, but he'd yet to delve into her thoughts and memories deep enough to find out what drove her. Could he protect her from herself?

"Would you look at that?" she said from the passenger seat.

Jack followed her line of sight to Black's Cove Lake. The mist had dissipated and the afternoon sun shone on its surface, hitting the water and creating glistening diamonds in ribbons of light.

"It's so beautiful."

"Yes, it is." He enjoyed the awe in her voice.

They drove the last quarter of a mile to the house and he pulled the car into the garage.

"Stuart will help me take care of my arm. Make yourself comfortable in the parlor."

He glanced over at her and saw a stubborn glint in her eyes. She clamped her teeth together, jutting her chin forward. He was in trouble.

"I'd like to help because it's my fault you were shot. I do realize now that if it's too good to be true, it probably isn't."

Maybe there was hope for her hard-nosed, got-to-have-the-truth-at-any-cost attitude after all.

Stuart stepped into the garage and opened the car door. "Sir, I received your call. How are you holding up?"

"Thanks to Miss Morgan's bandaging job I think I'm going to make it."

She climbed out and came around the nose of the car, catching his good arm with her hand.

Heat shot through him.

"You called him? When?"

"My car is equipped with an alarm. Stuart knew there'd been trouble a moment after it happened."

"Oh. How super-heroish."

Stuart stared at her hard and long and Jack felt tension ignite the air around them. "It's all right. Miss Morgan had some problems and I was forced to rectify them."

"Very well." He moved forward, opened the door into the house and followed them inside. "Will you need Mr. Smith?"

"No. It's a flesh wound. I'll take care of it in the lab."

Stuart preceded them through the kitchen and out into a narrow hallway. "If you need me, sir, I'll be outside."

Jack nodded to Stuart, reached for the knob and pulled the closet door open.

"You're kidding me, right?" Olivia whispered next to him, a tremor in her voice. "A secret lab?"

Amusement glided through him, but he held it in check. Every detail he gave her put him in danger of exposure and increased the fact that he couldn't allow her to leave.

"My grandfather had to protect his research." He took her hand and they stepped into the cubical. He shut the door and a tiny light came on overhead.

"On NPQ?"

"Yes."

"That's spooky."

Jack reached through the mass of hanging coats and pressed the elevator's Down button.

"I don't think you understand, Olivia."

"Then why don't you help me to?" She stared at him, her blue eyes sparkling in the dim light. The proximity of her body to his stirred primal need in his bloodstream. A knot fisted in his gut and he was forced to look away, taking his trail of desire with him. She was dangerous and in danger. It was a twisted equation that could get them both killed.

"His research was cutting-edge in the late seventies. There were other scientists working along the same lines, but my grandfather was the first and only one to perfect the formula—"

"And use it on human test subjects?"

He was digging his own grave. "Yes."

"My brother Ross…and you?"

"Yes." Maybe there was hope she'd believe they were the only two test subjects. Maybe he could contain the situation after all.

The elevator car landed with a soft jolt and Jack opened the door. Taking her hand, he led her out into his grandfather's lab and hit the light switch panel on the wall. Rows of fluorescent lights came to life, illuminating the pristine room, its walls lined with work areas, exam tables and shelves of chemicals and compounds.

"Do you use this place?"

He let go of her hand and retrieved the medical kit

from inside a cupboard. "I used to, after I graduated from medical school. But I realized I didn't want to follow in my grandfather's footsteps. The Foundation was doing good work and needed someone at its helm, so I changed my focus."

He laid the kit on one of the exam tables and opened it. Taking out a pressure dressing, swabs, sterile water, several gauze pads and some antiseptic, he laid everything out for her.

"Come on, I'll tell you what to do." He unbuttoned his shirt one-handed. "Take off the bandage."

Olivia felt the pull toward him well before she picked at the knot she'd tied in the makeshift dressing. Her heart hammered in her eardrums as she fiddled with the material and released the square knot. She unwound it, noting the bleeding had stopped almost completely. The lab gave her the creeps and she wondered what was behind the massive vault door in the far corner of the room. Did mad scientists have vaults where they kept their demented formulas?

"It looks good. No more bleeding."

"First aid training?" He pulled his good arm out of his shirt first and eased off the bloody sleeve on the other side.

Olivia swallowed and tried to keep her stare on the bullet wound rather than the broad expanse of his bare chest, but it wasn't easy. The whole room closed in on her.

"Yeah. I clean it up with antiseptic first." She tried to pull herself together.

"Yes. Use lots of it. I don't want this to get infected." He sat down on the exam table in front of her. Now she was forced to stare at his skin, hugging well-shaped pecs and pulled taut over ripped abs. Even the branching lines of scarring left her wanting to trace them with her fingertips.

Damn. She was in some kind of trouble.

She fumbled for the bottle of sterile water, grasping it as he reached for her chin and pulled her face up, making eye contact.

Her head spun.

"If this is a problem for you, Olivia, I can get someone else."

"It would help if you didn't…touch me, while I'm trying to work."

A sultry smile bowed his sexy lips and drained the reservoir of denial she was paddling around in. Her lifeboat sank and she leaned into him, caught in a current of raging desire she couldn't swim out of.

He took her mouth in complete possession, exploring her with his tongue in slow sensuous strokes that stoked the fire burning in her veins. Her body engorged with heat so hot that she thought she'd melt into her shoes. Then he let her go, grasping her upper arms to keep her from rocking over and falling backward.

His eyes narrowed as he studied her. "You said you hadn't been kissed enough after your near-death experience. I thought I'd take the opportunity to rectify that."

Suspicion took a hold of her jumbled physical and emotional faculties. She reached for a piece of gauze to clean around the wound. "You just want me to keep my mouth shut about your being the Phantom. That'll take care of it, Jack." She knew she was lying, as she twisted the cap off the bottle. Being kissed by him had only shown her how needy she really was, how behind her hard-charging style she was still a woman.

A woman without love in her life.

His teeth clamped together, setting a hard line along his jawbone.

What was his game? Did he really think seduction equaled no exposé? Did he think her heart was up for grabs? Well, he'd be wrong. She swallowed hard and doused the gauze with water.

Working carefully, she wiped the drying blood from around the wound at the entrance and exit sites. Thank God, it was a clean shot that had penetrated the skin on the underside of his upper arm. The bullet had missed the bone.

"Thank you." She looked him in the eyes. "Thank you for doing what you do and for making sure I survived."

"You're welcome."

She put the bloodied gauze down and picked up the iodine. "This might sting," she said as she saturated the swab and began probing the wound.

He didn't flinch, didn't look at her again until she'd slathered antibiotic cream on his arm and bandaged it.

Jack teetered on a precipice of his own making. He could let her go and his identity as the Phantom would be front-page news within the week, but that wasn't the worst of it. They would try to kill her again and they might succeed next time.

Or he could play his last card and force her to stay where he could protect her and convince her to let the story die.

"All done." She stepped back and he was hyper-aware of her body, of the curve of her full breasts pressing against the fabric of her torn blouse, of the pensive, what's-next way she held her mouth in a manner that belied her quick wit and active mind.

He slid off the exam table and stepped toward her. "I'll drive you back to the hotel, so you can get your things."

Her eyes widened. He prepared for an ardent protest.

"You're not safe and I won't have your blood on my hands."

Still, she just stared at him like he'd grown an eye in the middle of his forehead and sprouted horns.

"You can't keep me here!" Indignation spoiled her features and made his heart squeeze.

Jack reached for her, but she bolted out of his grasp.

Dammit, he'd do anything to keep her safe. Even endure her hatred. But he'd rather reason with her.

"You saw the power they possess. They tried to kill you this morning."

"Who are they?" She moved around him in a circle.

"I can't tell you. But I can promise you'll be safe here. They won't try to harm you while you're in my care."

"There are more like you…that's it." Her mouth opened in wonder. "They have the same power as you do."

"Not the same." His veil of secrecy was thinning a degree at a time.

"Enough." He moved toward the desk in the corner and pulled open the bottom drawer. Reaching inside he took out her red baseball cap, the one she'd dropped in the basement of the clinic. He hated to threaten her, but he was out of options. This was concrete. This was something she could understand, respect.

He turned around.

The force of something hard made contact with his head. Pain and anger, burned through him.

"You can't keep me here!" she yelled, raising the chair for a second blow.

Jack held out her red ball cap.

Olivia froze in mid-act. The meaning of the lost hat sinking deep into her brain. Jack had been there the first night she broke into the clinic and he'd been there the night the fire almost took her life. Jack Trayborne was the Phantom of Black's Cove. He held her fate in his hands. But he'd also saved her life time and again.

"You would use that against me? You would turn me in for breaking and entering?" She lowered the chair.

A bead of fear pearled inside of her, culturing hesitation. She could go to jail.

"Stay, Olivia."

"Do I have a choice?"

Chapter Eight

Jack stared at the lakefront cottage less than a hundred yards from the main house. He'd chosen to give her a space of her own. She'd accepted his ultimatum on the surface, but underneath he'd tapped into her resentment. She hated being trapped, feeling helpless…and scared. That wasn't his goal, to frighten her, but if it worked to keep her safe, it was a tactic he felt compelled to employ.

He glanced at the thick file in his hand and took the steps off the terrace. Maybe having access to Ross's medical information would alleviate her distress. Convince her the clinic had done everything short of curing him. Maybe then she'd consent to leaving Black's Cove for good.

Regret ticked along his nerves and matched the beat of his footsteps through the rose garden and onto the porch of the cottage. His approach alerted Gunner, his German shepherd, and he immediately rushed toward him, tail wagging.

Jack patted the dog's head and raised his hand to knock.

The door opened before he could rap on it.

"I saw you coming." She turned away leaving the door open for him to enter.

The sway of her hips in her blue jeans made his jaw clench and he pulled in a deep breath before crossing the threshold into the land of temptation.

"I have something for you."

She stopped, turned and plopped down on the couch, a devil-may-care grin on her face. "You're going to free me from this exquisitely decorated prison?"

A knot swelled in his chest. He lowered himself onto the chair facing the sofa.

"It's Ross's medical file."

She dropped the contrivance she'd wrapped herself in and sat forward. "You would give that to me?"

"Yes." He watched disbelief pull her eyebrows together as she studied him, her intense blue-eyed gaze never leaving his face.

"It's that simple. You give me the medical file, I read through it, determine if the clinic is responsible for his present medical condition and I'm good to go?"

"Something like that."

The briefest flash of acceptance flitted across her pleasing features and he moved in for the kill.

"There's one condition. You leave Black's Cove immediately and you leave its secrets behind when you go. You'll have the answers you seek about Ross and I'll have my anonymity. There will be no exposé. Do we have an agreement?"

Reluctance kept him out of her mind. Any trail of thought she went down could only lead him back to his belief that she thought he was a freak and she'd love nothing better than to expose him as one.

Olivia stood up, her nerves a jumbled mass of short-circuiting bio-matter. What Jack was asking was career suicide for her, a lethal dose of unemployment. A journalist who couldn't dish was dead. Was she willing to trade the story of the century for a manila file with her brother's name on it?

Remnants of guilt surfaced in her mind, dragging her toward a decision. She stared at the folder Jack held so casually. He had her recompense in his hands. The absolution of her guilt for causing the accident that injured Ross.

"You know I have to take Ross's file."

"Yes, but why, Olivia? Why are you willing to risk your life for what's inside this folder?" He held it out to her.

A lump formed in her throat. She reached for the information, but he pulled it back. "Why is this so important to you?"

The sting of tears blazed behind her eyelids. She wanted to run, wanted to escape his scrutiny as badly as she wanted to avoid her own.

"Because Ross's accident was my fault. He was on my trike and I wanted it back, so I pushed him. He was two." Her voice cracked and she turned loose of the pent-up pain festering inside of her.

"I was only four, for God's sake! I had no idea he

would roll so fast into the street. My mother tried to catch him, but she couldn't and then the car…"

Jack advanced on her and pulled her into his arms. She didn't resist; she didn't have the will to. She needed to feel his touch, his sympathy, his consolation and she wasn't disappointed.

She listened to the drum of his heartbeat under her ear and closed her eyes, letting the tears come.

He brushed his hand over her head, pressing her tightly against him.

"You had no way of knowing what would happen, Olivia. Children lack reasoning skills and understanding of the consequences of their actions. Their cognitive function hasn't fully developed at that age."

His justification made perfect neurological sense, but there wasn't much emotional solace in it.

She pulled back and dabbed at her eyes with the sleeve of her shirt. "I sabotaged my own childhood. From that day on, we traipsed around the country looking for help. Some miracle cure for his brain damage. My parents barely looked at me after that and never forgave me. They're both dead now, my dad twelve years ago, and my mom a year ago."

Her throat squeezed shut, and it took every ounce of strength she had not to bust up again. "Ross is my responsibility."

Jack moved her to the couch and sat down next to her. He had his answer. Knew what drove her; why she did what she did, why she wrapped herself in a shell of invincibility. She needed forgiveness. Not from Ross, not from her deceased parents, but from herself and he doubted she was going to find it in her brother's medical file.

"Take it." He held out the folder. "There's enough in here to convince you Black's Cove Clinic did everything possible to help your brother, but he didn't respond to the treatment." He laid the file on the coffee table and reached for her chin with his fingers, tipping up her face.

"It was a tragic accident, Olivia. You're no more to blame than I was for my parents' car accident. Forgive yourself. Move past it."

If his words touched her at all it didn't show in her eyes or the pull of her mouth. He let go of her and felt the void open between them.

"If only it was that simple." She turned out of his grasp, picked up the file and stood up. "I'll return this to you ASAP."

She disappeared into the bedroom and closed the door.

Jack stood up, feeling discontent pulse in his blood. He couldn't expect years of guilt and resentment to dry up in a matter of minutes.

He turned for the door, knowing it was going to take longer for her to forgive herself and drop the facade she hid her heart behind. In that respect, they were very much alike.

OLIVIA STEPPED OUT of the cottage onto the porch and turned her attention toward the main house. Her gut-wrenching admission to Jack an hour ago had left her feeling torn. Unpacking her emotional baggage on his doorstep was risky, but she'd seen the sympathy in his eyes. Genuine? Yes. But could she take his advice and forgive herself?

Gunner took off like a shot for the driveway, warning her that someone or something had roused him from the doggie bed next to the cottage's front door. So much for staying around to guard her.

She closed the door and headed across the expansive lawn to investigate the commotion. If nothing else, she intended to bring Gunner back with her. She kind of liked the ninety-pound puppy with razor-sharp teeth, a tail that wagged at the sound of her voice and a master who had trained him to protect on command.

Go to the lake.

Olivia stopped, unsure where the wayward thought had come from. Granted, she wanted to take a walk out onto the dock for a look around, but now wasn't the time.

A chill brushed across her skin and penetrated her body. She shuddered and turned around, her gaze drawn to the lake's edge, to the dock rocking gently in the ripples driven by the breeze.

Come to the water.

She took a step forward, then another.

Gunner's piercing bark broke the odd trance she found herself in and she stepped back.

What the hell was happening?

She had to find Gunner.

Olivia turned and jogged forward, pausing when she heard the sound of voices near the right side of the house, the spot where she'd last seen the dog.

"You can't keep her here! She needs to leave, before she destroys us all." The female's voice hit a note of recognition inside of Olivia's head and caution sang through her.

It was the same woman who'd called her this morning and lured her into the path of an oncoming freight train.

Ducking in next to the corner of the house behind a juniper bush, she went still, watching Jack and the woman carry a large box past her hiding place and stop next to a koi pond in the middle of the yard.

"I have it under control, but I need to know if you tried to hurt her again this morning by forcing her car into the 11:55?"

"No!"

The woman's high-pitched denial ground over Olivia's nerves. Anger flared inside of her, ignited by a shot of betrayal. No one controlled her, but she wondered if they were in on it together? Had Jack somehow been involved in trying to kill her to shut her up? Normally she was great at untwisting the spin. Maybe venting to Jack had weakened her position, made her vulnerable…easy to manipulate.

"I haven't gone near her since you stopped us from mowing her down on Main Street."

Olivia put the flame of anger out in favor of eavesdropping, even though she really wanted to smack the shapely brunette in the teeth for lying.

"What about Rick?"

"I don't keep tabs on him. You'll have to ask him yourself."

"I will." He bent over and opened the top of the box. "I can get this, Diana. I'll see you next week with the rest."

"Are you sure?" She stepped close to him, reached out and put her hand on his arm.

Olivia recoiled, suddenly consumed with an emotion that made her mad all over. Jealousy?

"Why don't you come to me anymore, Jack?"

He straightened and took a step back.

Olivia's cheeks heated, every nerve ending in her body frayed, spilling information she didn't want to accept, much less witness. There was familiarity between the two of them. It made her bristle.

"I can't anymore."

"But we need each other. We're alike."

Alike? Horror surged in Olivia's veins, her stare going to the woman's flip-flop-clad feet, to a spot on her left ankle where three distinctive black dots could be seen.

She was one of the test subjects from the clinic? She had the mark and abilities like Jack's?

His jaw clenched, he pulled his shoulders back and crossed his arms over his chest. "I won't be back."

"Are you sure about that, Jack?" She stepped toward him, a seductive sway to the movement of her hips. "You liked it once."

Olivia nearly gave up her hiding place to charge in, but she pulled back. Did kissing him give her the right to object?

Jack reached out and caught Diana by the upper arms. He squeezed until he saw her eyes widen. His decision was final, although he didn't know why the woman he'd once lusted after no longer held any appeal in his mind or for his body.

"Leave, Diana, and don't come back. And if you ever try to hurt her again…I'll make sure it's the last thing you ever do."

He released her. She rocked back, dusting at her arms where he'd touched her.

"You don't frighten me, Jack. She's made you fuzzy in the head. We'll all go down if you don't do something. I've got milking to do at the shop. Call me when you come to your senses."

He turned back to his task, ignoring her as she strode across the lawn toward the driveway.

Releasing Diana was something he should have done long ago, and just the thought of touching her ever again left him stone-cold.

Dipping into the lined box, he netted the first koi, and released it into the pond. Catching its mate, he put it into the water and watched it swim away, disappearing into the murky depths.

He had Olivia to thank for his newfound need. Kissing her the first time had been spontaneous. Doing it a second time had negated his resistance. Now he wanted more. So much more.

"Who was that, Jack?"

Surprised for the first time in a long time, he swung around to find Olivia standing a couple of feet away. She stood with her fists at her sides, ready to fight. Tension tightened her features and sent warning currents rippling out around her.

"What's wrong?"

"That woman, you know her?"

"Yes."

"She's the one who called my cell this morning and lured me into the path of the train. I recognize her voice."

Caution slipped down his spine and fanned out across his nerves. What was Diana's game?

"You're sure?"

"What is she to you, Jack?"

"Nothing that can't be remedied."

"Where does she live? I'm going to interrogate her. Find out what's going on. Find out why she tried to kill me."

"Hold on, Olivia." Jack dropped the net and stepped in front of her, blocking her path.

"I'll take you. Just promise you'll calm down and you won't charge in."

"Why?"

"She's dangerous."

She stared up at him, her features softening as understanding undid her resolve.

"She's like you."

"Yes."

"YOU'RE KIDDING ME." Olivia tried to relax on the seat next to Jack, but it was impossible as she stared at the Exotic Pet Shop sign hanging over the door. "And I thought she was going to milk cows or something."

Her attempt at humor didn't faze Jack and he

wouldn't even crack a smile, a fact that bothered her. Somewhere inside the obscure shop at the end of Main Street was a milking room filled with deadly king cobras.

"Next you're going to tell me her special abilities allow her to handle venomous snakes without being bitten."

"Something like that." He climbed out of the car and she did the same, following him across the street.

It was 6:00 p.m. and most of the shops were already closed, their blinds drawn.

They made the sidewalk at the precise moment a young girl opened the pet shop door, stepped outside and turned to lock it.

"Molly?"

She started and whirled around, her hand going to her heart. "Oh, Mr. Trayborne, you scared me."

"Is Diana inside?"

"Yeah, she's in the milking room."

"I need to speak with her."

"Sure." She pivoted and reinserted the key, unlocking the shop door. "Just turn the dead bolt once you're inside."

"Thanks." Jack took Olivia's hand and pulled her into the shop, heightening his senses before he turned the dead bolt and waved at Molly through the glass.

Caution sang along his nerves as he moved through the dimly lit room, glancing down the store aisles as he moved past, aiming for the door into the back.

A high-pitched hiss hit his eardrums. He lunged for the door. He'd heard that sound once before while helping Diana milk cobra venom for the Trayborne

Research Labs in Atlanta and L.A. It was distinctive to a king cobra in a defense mode.

He paused at the door and squeezed Olivia's hand. "Something's wrong, stay close."

Olivia beat back the creepy crawlies with the knowledge that Jack was beside her. She had her very own Phantom protector and she wished like crazy he'd shield them in an energy field like he did to stop the bullets because more than any slimy creature on earth, she hated snakes.

Jack turned the knob and ease the door open. Terror forced her heart rate up and she clung to him as he pushed through the door and into a large room.

In the center was a glass cubical.

Diana lay sprawled on the floor, an agitated cobra inches from her body, hood deployed, his body coiled to deliver another strike.

Jack let go of her hand. "She's barely alive! Get the antivenom hypodermic out of the cooler in the corner. It's banded in red."

She hurried to the refrigerator and pulled it open, spotting the syringe.

Movement, long, dark and fast, sliced across the peripheral field of vision on her left. She whirled around.

"Snake!" But her warning came too late.

The reptile reared a fraction and lunged at Jack, catching him on the leg.

Olivia yanked the lid off the large trash can next to the fridge and picked it up.

Pain slammed into Jack's body, taking his breath

with it. Realization pounded in his brain and he reached for the cobra, raising it up off the floor in a beam of telekinetic energy.

He could feel the effects of the neurotoxin entering his blood stream and fanning out over his body. He didn't have much time.

"In here!" Olivia shouted, moving closer with the trash can. "Put him in here!"

Jack lowered the snake into the can and collapsed against the door to the milking room just as she slammed on the lid.

"9-1-1," he tried to focus, feeling his diaphragm muscles begin to fail. "Call 9-1-1."

She rushed to Jack's side and folded on the ground next to him. Jerking up the sleeve on his shirt, she pulled the cap off the needle with her teeth. She had no idea what the hell she was doing; she worked on instinct.

"In the vein?" Jack's eyes rolled back in his head. She slapped his cheek with her free hand.

"Yes. In half an inch…that should do it."

She said a prayer and pushed the needle into Jack's arm.

Catching the top of the plunger with her thumb, she eased the clear liquid into his arm, pulled the needle and sat back.

He would live or he wouldn't, but every cell in her body needed him to survive. She'd be toast without him.

"Toast?" Jack said as he dragged open his eyes, feeling the load of bricks lift off his chest.

The antivenom was working. Olivia's quick thinking had saved his life. But Diana…

Straining to hear, he listened for her heartbeat. Nothing. "She's dead."

Olivia's head drooped forward, before she looked back up at him.

His breath caught in his throat. She was the most beautiful thing he'd seen in a long time and he reached out to her.

She huddled next to him and he closed his eyes, feeling his strength return from the neurotoxin cocktail the cobra had injected.

He'd never known Diana to make a mistake with the deadly snakes. She always used her telekinetic energy to manipulate them and erase her risk of being bitten. So how had it happened tonight? Had she lost focus for an instant? Or had someone else interfered?

"I need to cage the snakes. Call 9-1-1."

Reluctantly, she pulled back from Jack and helped him stand. She watched in awe as he reached out his hand and lifted the cobra from next to Diana's body, floating it in midair, up and back into its glass case.

Looking away she spotted the telephone on the wall next to the door and walked toward it.

They would never know why Diana had lured her onto the tracks, but she did know one thing for certain.

She cared for Jack Trayborne.

Chapter Nine

Olivia toweled her wet hair and slipped a robe on over her pink skin. She'd let the hot water blast her for half an hour, but she still couldn't rid herself of the chills.

Diana had been pronounced dead at the scene. That was a given considering she'd been bitten more than five times and it was doubtful that even the syringe of anti-venom she'd administered to Jack would have saved Diana's life. Another small fact continued to contribute to her state of worry.

One of the deadly king cobras was still missing.

A shudder ripped through her and she hugged her arms around her body as she left the bathroom and headed for the kitchen and a cup of cocoa to break the chill.

Gunner lay next to the front door. He raised his head when he saw her.

She'd grown quite attached to the big lug since Jack had demanded she keep him with her at all times. Considering the turn of events lately, maybe it wasn't such a bad idea. Another line of defense in a battle of invisible phenomena she'd yet to get her head around, wasn't a bad idea.

Opening the pantry, she stepped inside and rummaged a doggie treat out of its box, before grabbing a packet of hot chocolate.

A growl, low and ominous raised the hair at her nape. She stepped out of the pantry and closed the door.

"Gunner?" Taking cautious steps, she eased around the corner and stared at the German shepard. His ears were erect and he sat watching the door, a growl rumbling in his throat.

Olivia's stomach tightened and she reached for the phone. Something was out there. She didn't want to know what.

Come to the water.

JACK MOVED THROUGH the trees, cognizant of every sound emanating from the woods near the cottage. He attempted to blend in with the darkness, to become one with the element of cover surrounding him.

His nerves had been on edge since they'd returned from town, and the foreboding had only grown stronger as night set in, so he'd chosen to patrol, to pace, to watch, rather than rest.

Now he stared at the front door as the porch light flipped on.

Was she as restless as he was? Caught up in thoughts that drove sleep away and churned desire deep inside his bones?

He heard the door latch click open in amplified decibels.

Caution and worry stretched over him. It wasn't safe for her to go out.

Gunner hustled out the door, and stood at attention, his snout thrust up into the night air.

Jack pulled in a breath. What had alerted the dog? He scanned the darkness, catching movement on the far side of the cottage. But whoever it was vanished before he could get a clear fix on their location or intended direction.

He stepped out of the trees, moving across the lawn toward the threat.

The clouds parted, unmasking the half moon overhead. It illuminated the grounds, taking away his cover.

Jack froze in place, watching Olivia step through the front door of the cottage.

What was she doing? She shouldn't be out. He moved toward her, watching her stride along the path leading to the lake.

"Olivia!" he shouted.

No response. Her almost-robotic movements were worrisome.

Concern lengthened his strides.

She reached for the belt on her robe and untied it in slow motion. Peeling the garment off, she dropped it on the ground and continued her move toward the water.

His mouth went dry, his body churning up a desire hot enough to scorch metal.

Moonlight illuminated her naked skin and wet hair, shading and highlighting the curves of her body.

"Olivia. Stop!"

She reached the dock and walked the length of it, her trance-like state impervious to his voice.

Jack broke into a run. He reached out and surrounded her in a field of energy. Panic consumed him as he raised his hands, drawing her toward him several feet off the ground.

The moment she touched down, she jerked awake, staring at him with her mouth open, until she realized she didn't have any clothes on.

He snagged her robe off the grass and handed it to her. "What are you doing out here?"

"I don't know…. It's freezing." She shoved her arms into her robe and yanked the belt tight.

"Do you sleep walk?"

"No."

Caution inched through him and he pulled her toward the cottage.

Gunner's agitated whine bristled the hairs on his neck. He'd trained the dog to be sensitive to paranormal energy.

Telepathic manipulation. They were dealing with planted orders in the mind. Her mind. But who had that kind of power? Diana and the other test subjects, with the exception of Ross, were all dead. Which left Rick Dowdy?

Jack hurried her and Gunner inside and closed the door, locking it. She couldn't stay in the cottage any longer. She couldn't be left alone. He didn't want to frighten her, but things had just become measurably more dangerous.

"What do you remember, Olivia?"

Her cheeks were red, whether from embarrassment or the cold, he wasn't sure.

"I got out some cocoa…and a treat for Gunner. He started to growl at the door, and I decided to call you. I went for the phone and the next thing I remember, I was standing butt-naked outside, freezing to death."

"You were headed for the water."

She shuddered and he pulled her into his arms. The contact melted his defenses and fired his desire.

"I believe someone used telepathic manipulation on you and forced you to do something you wouldn't normally do."

She pulled back from him. "This afternoon when Diana was here, she denied coming near me since the accident on Main Street, but she was the one who called me this morning. What if someone used the same force on her?"

Her observation made sense, but it also drove a wedge of caution deep into his soul. If anyone around them could be manipulated to harm her, he'd have to ramp up his guard.

"Collect your things. You're moving into the main house."

She glared at him, but turned away and went into the bedroom to pack her suitcase.

Did she understand just how dangerous it was for her to be alone? Somehow he doubted it. The invincibility of her facade hadn't yet sustained enough cracks and he prayed it never did, even though he could feel several beginning to open up in his.

OLIVIA MOVED DOWN the stairs, curious about the commotion in the expansive entryway below.

Frances and Muriel chatted with another woman in a business suit and carrying a notepad, about flowers and food and other things she couldn't make out.

She reached the bottom of the stairs, glided past unnoticed and headed for the dining room and a cup of coffee, knowing she'd find Jack there before she turned the corner.

She'd read and reread Ross's medical file, but it hadn't gotten her any closer to the new answers she craved. Jack had blacked out the good stuff, a fact that only made her want to know more.

How many of them were there and why hadn't NPQ worked on Ross?

"Good morning," Jack said, looking up from his newspaper.

"Good morning. What's going on out there?" She pointed over her shoulder and proceeded to the sideboard for a cup of java.

"The Trayborne Foundation's annual masquerade charity ball is in two weeks. I always let Frances and Muriel handle the details."

"Mm." She sipped the blazing-hot coffee and set the cup down on the table to Jack's left. For emphasis, she tossed the medical file down next to her mug and pulled out her chair.

Jack looked at the manila folder and back up at her. "You found what you were looking for?"

"Sort of." She sat down and stared at him, watching his expressive blue eyes narrow. She'd cataloged his repertoire of expressions and knew she had his attention.

"You blacked out all the good stuff, Jack. I did learn that the clinic did all it could for Ross. He never responded to the treatment, so it's off the hook. What I don't know is what exactly NPQ consists of and what its side effects are."

"That's because my grandfather's studies ended."

"Why?"

Jack's expression hardened and he leaned back in his chair. She was losing him. That or he was clamming up to cover up. Her money was on the latter.

"Did the results terrify him, Jack? Did the test subjects manifest with paranormal powers that were dangerous, forcing him to scrap the entire line of research before it got out of hand?"

Tension bound her muscles in tight little knots. That was it. The research had gotten out of control.

"Before you make any judgments, Olivia, you must know that the NPQ program was halted by my grandfather because he knew the world wasn't ready for it. That the formula could be abused and create havoc if he allowed it to be marketed."

"So he hid it?" Excitement surged through her.

Jack's teeth clenched, his jaw turning rigid with anger that became palpable in the air around them.

Olivia swallowed, realizing the nerve she'd sliced into had deep roots inside Jack. His reaction frightened her, but kept her thoughts on the path of questioning she'd stumbled down.

He was the gatekeeper. The guardian of Pandora's box.

Fear radiated from her marrow and leeched into her bloodstream. The truth she'd been determined to uncover wasn't the one she'd expected. This truth carried with it overwhelming implications that, if applied, could tear the world apart.

"Glad you finally understand, Olivia."

She glanced at him, reality dawning hard and fast. "You can read my thoughts?"

"Yes. But I rarely do. I find it invasive, a violation of the solace afforded to everyone, the privacy of one's own mind. Do you understand now? Do you see why I can't allow you to expose any of this?"

"How many, Jack? How many are there?"

"Seven. Including myself. But four are dead, including Diana."

She understood now. Knew why he protected the truth. To allow exposure threatened everyone. The vault in the lab, that's where he kept it. Safe, protected…impenetrable? She shook off the cover of foreboding she felt weighing her down in light of Jack's revelation.

"I think I should leave. Go back home and take care of Ross."

He took her hand in his. He tried to smile, but she could see the level of worry in his eyes, feel its evasive presence coil around her heart.

"I wish it were that simple now, Olivia. But it's not…not until I find and confront whoever's behind this. I've come to the conclusion that he plans to eliminate anyone who gets in his way, anyone who tries to stop him or expose the truth, including you."

Jack's heart expanded in his chest. He brushed his hand along her cheek, feeling the charge arc between them and jolt his emotions to life. They'd been idle too long. Imprisoned inside a narrow vein, buried out of reach.

The echo of voices sucked him back into reality, as Frances led Muriel and Isadora Collins, the party planner, into the dining room.

Jack let his hand drop from Olivia's face, but kept his gaze on her. Her cheeks flamed a sensuous color of pink that made his mouth water.

"In here I'd like the punch, hors d'oeuvres, pastries and a cluster of tall tables." Frances waved her hand at the expansive room, pausing when she saw him and Olivia sitting at the table. "Oh, I'm sorry, sir. I had no idea you were still in here."

"Not a problem. Miss Morgan and I were just about to leave for a trip into town."

"Very well, sir. Be assured things are coming along quite nicely." Frances smiled and showed the other two women back out into the hallway.

"This must be some kind of shindig."

"It's the Foundation's single-most important fund-raising event." He reached inside his jacket pocket and pulled out a foiled envelope. Laying it on the table, he slid it over to her and sat back.

Olivia's hand shook as she reached for the invitation. Even Cinderella got to go to the ball.

She picked it up and broke the wax seal pressed with an elaborate *T*. Opening the flap, she pulled out the simple white parchment card, scrolled on in black script. It was official, she'd be attending the masquerade ball.

Jack's gaze never left her face and she heated under his intense scrutiny. "I'd love to go, but I've nothing to wear."

A sly grin bowed his mouth and she found her stare transfixed on his lips. Longing spread through her and brought her to her feet. If she left the room now she could avoid the overwhelming desire tempting her to kiss him, but she didn't want to resist the need.

"Then don't." He stood up, too, and pulled her into his arms. His mouth came down on hers with a tender force that robbed her of conscious thought.

In brazen delight, she closed her eyes, feeling the level of his desire as he pressed his body to hers.

"Yes," she mentally whispered.

Jack pulled her up into his arms, breaking the kiss as he stared down at her with eyes the color of blazing sapphires. "Are you sure?" The husky note in his voice fanned the flames inside of her and they roared out of control.

She nodded, consumed with primal need that clawed for satisfaction.

He found her lips again before he carried her out of

the dining room, down the hallway and up the stairs. Every encounter, every kiss, every touch has been leading them to this moment of fulfillment.

Olivia relaxed in his arms, feeling his strength holding her. Why she'd ever believed she could live without someone to care for, she couldn't imagine.

Jack slowed his pace, even though he felt like running to the bedroom. Every inch of his body was primed to make love to her again and again. To satisfy the desire that burned through the last remnants of his control.

He stepped through the bedroom door and kicked it shut with his foot.

The house echoed with the sound.

Moving to the bed, he set her down beside it and began the slow process of undressing her. Her breath came in heavy gasps. He trailed kisses along her shoulder, feeling her body respond to his touch, lips on naked skin.

His heartbeat thundered in his eardrums, pounding out a rhythm of excitement. All other thought melted away as he stared at her beautiful body.

He stripped off his clothes and pulled back the sheet. Together, they climbed into bed and he pulled the covers up over their heads, entombing them in a cocoon.

Olivia knew she'd died and gone to heaven because she'd never been touched like this before. Reaching up, she splayed her hand against the back of Jack's head, forcing his mouth down on her left breast. A moan escaped from between her parted lips as he pulled her nipple into his mouth, ringing it with his tongue, before pulling back to stare down at her, a seductive smile on his face.

Reaching out, he traced his finger around her other nipple, then dragged it down her belly. She pushed against him as he slid his entire hand down to cover her before massaging her with his finger.

Heat burned through her, driving her temperature up and pushing her closer to the fire.

"Please." She mentally begged him, glad when he pulled her underneath him, trailing kisses across her forehead as he pressed against her.

"Are you sure, Olivia?" he asked again.

She stared up at him, at the piece of wayward hair against his forehead, at the gleam in his dark blue eyes. She reached up and touched his cheek, feeling the thin layer of perspiration on his skin. "I need you."

"We need each other," he whispered.

She opened for him.

Exerting control he didn't feel, he penetrated her, feeling her warmth surround him. Deeper and deeper until he filled her completely.

The sound of her heartbeat drummed in his ears, her soft sighs evoking waves of pleasure as he moved inside of her harder and faster. Each stroke driving them both closer to the ultimate satisfaction.

She climaxed beneath him. He raised up, driving into her with deep thrusts. She cried out in ecstasy.

He followed her, pumping until he came, spilling himself inside of her in waves.

Gradually he stopped and pulled out of her. Rolling

over, he took her in his arms, burying his face in her hair, breathing her in.

It was so much better than in his precognitive vision. He planned to keep that detail from her. Her sense of right would find it totally wrong that he'd known this would happen. Had welcomed it, needed it…but there was more, so much more he couldn't analyze.

He had to figure out how to save her first.

Chapter Ten

Jack maneuvered the Jaguar out onto the main road and headed for Black's Cove with Olivia next to him. Making love to her had only deepened the degree of his concern. From now on, they were joined at the hip. Where she went, he'd go; where he went, she'd come.

"Look, Jack, I don't want you to get the wrong idea about me. I don't normally act like that. I'm not easy...I just—"

"Leave it alone, Olivia. Don't overanalyze it. We enjoyed being together."

"Okay." She stared out the window, seeing and not seeing the woods as they blitzed by. Caring about Jack Trayborne was all she seemed to have done for the last couple of hours, but it was clear he didn't want her to.

Jack slowed the car for a series of sharp turns down off the plateau where the estate sat. The narrow, tree-lined road was the only treacherous piece of highway between the house and Black's Cove.

The first curve was the worst. He pressed down on the brake pedal. The car slowed and rolled into the sweeping corner.

In the middle of his lane, stood a man in a black ski mask, hands outstretched.

Jack reacted, yanking hard to the left on the wheel. He pulled it right to swerve back into his lane.

The car didn't respond.

A blade of reality sliced through his body. They were going to crash.

Instinctively, he cast energy around them, but found a barrier blocking his own body.

The car shot off the edge of the road.

Seconds ticked by like hours. Metal twisted, glass shattered, its noise filling the interior compartment.

The car rolled over and over, scooping up tree branches, rocks and debris that churned in the momentum with them, as they spiraled down the steep two-hundred-foot decline into a ravine, landing upside down in a shallow creek.

Olivia sucked in a ragged breath, her equilibrium still on spin cycle.

Her seat belt held her in place, cutting into her lower abdomen, but she wasn't hurt. Trying to focus, she fiddled for the latch, found it and released herself head first into ten inches of icy water rushing through the upside-down car.

Raising herself onto her hands and knees, she shoved her soaking wet hair out of her eyes, seeing Jack for the first time.

"Jack!" Panic released adrenaline in her veins and she reached out to touch him.

He hung unconscious in the driver's seat. What had happened? Why hadn't he protected himself?

"Talk to me, Jack," she begged, working to free him.

Blood ran from a deep gash on the side of his head and she halted her efforts. If he had a neck injury, she could make it worse. She had to get help.

She spotted the cell phone on his belt and pulled it out of its holder. Her hands shook as she opened the phone and dialed 9-1-1.

"9-1-1 dispatch, what is your emergency?"

"We've gone off the road on Highway 21, about five miles from—"

The phone jerked out of her hand and slammed into the door casing, shattering into pieces.

Fear climbed up her spine as she scanned the area around the car.

Brush cracked, a series of small rocks rolled down the steep hillside and slammed into the car.

It was him, the man she'd seen standing in the middle of the road. She was sure he'd caused the car to go over the edge and now he wanted to make sure they were dead?

Reaching out she patted Jack's cheek. "Come on, Jack, you've got to wake up. Come on…come on." She had to get him out of the wreckage. They had to hide.

Olivia looked around for any kind of a weapon and saw a thick limb that they'd picked up in the mayhem.

Grabbing it, she submerged it in the water and sat up, leaning her head against the back of the upside-down seat.

She went perfectly still and closed her eyes, willing her shivering body to quit. If he stopped to check her pulse, she'd let him have it.

Awareness hit Jack like a sledge hammer, starting with his head. The fact that he was hanging upside down didn't help either. They'd been catapulted off the road intentionally. Someone wanted both of them dead.

He opened one eye and turned his head, spotting Olivia leaning against the seat next to him. He heightened his senses, hearing the frantic beat of her heart. She was uninjured, he knew, because he'd protected her. So why was she overly agitated?

"Olivia."

Her eyes blinked open and she put her finger to her lips, asking for silence. She reached up and patted her head.

Jack immediately reached into her mind, hearing her plea for silence, hearing her warning that he was coming down the embankment to make sure he'd killed both of them.

Caution lit in his veins. He reached up, found his seat belt and surrounded himself in a bubble just before he released it. He made a soft landing, released the energy field and turned to sit upright.

"We're sitting ducks here, Olivia. We've got to get out, so we can maneuver."

"But he's almost on top of us."

Jack reached out and took her hand, feeling electricity zap up his arm. "Let's go."

They crawled out the driver's window and onto the bank of the creek.

Combing the surrounding woods, Jack searched for their tormenter's location, pinpointing him halfway up the hillside.

Who were they dealing with? Did he have the same level of power? Jack was almost certain it wasn't Rick Dowdy edging his way toward them.

A thick stand of pines fifty feet away would serve as a shield for anything he directed at them.

"The trees," he said, motioning toward the cluster and encased them in a protective bubble.

Jack's head throbbed as he stood up and took off for the shelter. He'd made the trip down the hillside without the benefit of protection. How the man had accomplished that gave Jack pause. Were his abilities multifaceted? Or did they mirror his own?

He pulled Olivia into the shelter of pines and released the shield. "Whatever you do, stay behind these trees. He's strong, Olivia."

Fear bunched her features as she stared at him. Stretching up onto her tiptoes, she found his lips.

The kiss was sweet, lingering on his mouth long after she pulled back.

He had to protect her, had to keep her safe.

The grind of metal in motion drew his attention. Jack leaned out, shooting a glance toward the creek bed.

The crushed Jaguar floated two feet off the ground, slowly turning upright. He was looking for their bodies in the wreckage.

He couldn't see him, but Jack anticipated his next action and pinned Olivia against a tree.

The car shot forward and smashed broadside into the wall of timber five feet off the ground.

Olivia's startled shriek echoed in the woods around them and razed the last of Jack's control.

Reaching out he forced the twisted car to the ground with their attacker's hold still on it. Their energy fields collided, sending a shower of sparks flying.

He was strong, a fact that pushed Jack to the brink of losing control. Fear laced through him and held his emotions in check. He'd never pushed himself out of bounds, feared what would happen if he did. Could he pull back his control?

Anger churned inside of him, igniting rage in his body that emanated from his very core.

"Don't come out, Olivia," he warned.

Her eyes went wide as she stared up at him and he almost reached up to see if he'd turned into some sort of monster.

She brushed his arm as he stepped out from the cover of the trees and raised his hands.

Like an explosion being released, he detonated inside, sending a wall of energy up the slope, stripping the underbrush, pine needles and leaves from the trees in a rush.

There, standing exposed was the man in the black ski mask.

Rage fueled his emotions, even as his mind worked to bring them under control.

He cast a beam of energy around the stranger, roping him in its knot. He raised him ten feet off the ground and dragged him forward.

He'd remove the mask, find out who they were dealing with and crush the life out of him.

Olivia's scream of terror blasted against his eardrums and penetrated his brain.

She hung suspended five feet to his left, held in a beam of energy coming from the masked man. But how was it possible? How was the stranger able to function from inside the bubble?

Reality jolted him, zapping through his body in waves of knowledge that terrified him.

He released the beam and watched the man fall, catching himself before he hit the ground.

In that instance of misdirection, Jack took control over Olivia, encasing her and pushing her back behind the trees. He followed her into the shelter and put her down.

"You can't win, Jack!"

Jack stilled, employing his ability to mind sweep, reaching inside the attacker's head for information, but he found a wall he couldn't penetrate.

"Nice try, but it won't work. I'm more powerful than you'll ever be!"

For an instant, he hesitated, searching for reason in a scenario that seemed to lack one. This was an exercise in abilities. A fact-finding fight. It paid to know your enemy.

"What do you want?"

The sound of a siren in the distance and closing fast echoed from the roadway above.

He stared out at the masked attacker, watched him glance toward the road, step back and retreat toward the woods.

Again, he reached for the man's thoughts, catching a trail this time.

They would never be safe. No one in Black's Cove was safe...

A wave of excruciating pain hit Jack like a hammer between the eyes.

He rocked back, his stomach churning, sure his head was about to implode. He leaned against a broad tree trunk to keep from falling over.

He planned to cause Jack so much trouble he'd beg him to make the trade.... Her life for the.... The thread was lost, and Jack went to his knees.

"YOU'VE GOT A concussion and some swelling in your brain, Jack. You're fortunate it isn't worse." Doctor Perkins shoved his hands in the pockets of his coat. "I'm going to keep you overnight for observation, if it's better by morning, you can go home."

Olivia felt her agitation ramp up along with Jack's. What had happened to them this morning was disturbing, especially the fact that Jack had been unable to best the maniac flinging the car around like it was a toothpick.

Fear welled in her veins and spread its toxic mixture through her body. Jack was her only hope, her only defense against a power she was just beginning to understand.

"I'd like to sedate you, to keep outside impulses at a low level. Give your brain time to recover."

"No. I don't want to be sedated."

"If we don't, you'll need to remain immobile."

"I understand." His mouth pulled into a grim hard line, injecting an ounce of fear into her.

"What will happen if he doesn't obey orders?" she asked.

"He could have a stroke…. He could die. Any number of very serious results could occur."

Olivia swallowed the lump in her throat and stared at Jack, wondering if it was possible for a protector like him to care about himself for once?

"He'll do it and I'll help make sure he does."

Jack's eyes narrowed. "I know what's at stake. I'll give you one night, Doctor Perkins."

"Good." He slipped Jack's medical chart into the holder at the foot of the bed and left the room.

"Why so stubborn?" Olivia pulled the drape around Jack's bed and sat down on the edge, lowering her voice to a whisper. "Does this have anything to do with him?"

Jack nodded. "No one in Black's Cove is safe. He threatened them. This is my community. These are my people. I can't let him hurt them."

Olivia reached out and stroked her hand down the side of Jack's face breaking his intense mood.

He closed his eyes and turned into her palm, finding it with his lips before he gazed up at her.

"How are you going to help them if you're dead, Jack?"

Her question turned his full attention on her. Warmth moved through her like liquid fire. His hot blue gaze left little doubt he was thinking about the way they'd spent their morning, not the last three hours.

"Do what the doc says. Kick back and relax. Let your brain heal. I'll stay right here." What he really needed was to relinquish control. Hand it over for just one night.

"I won't let anything happen to you," she promised.

He reached up and cupped her hand where it rested on his cheek. His features softened, letting go of the tension that had been obvious moments ago.

"I'll hold you to it." He closed his eyes.

Olivia pulled her hand back, stood up and slid a chair close to Jack's bed.

She watched him slip into la-la land, tracing imaginary fingertips along the edge of his strong jaw. Brushing the piece of wayward hair off his forehead and joining it with the rest at his temple.

When had she given her heart away to him? When had her drive to get the story waned and turned to the desire to care for Jack Trayborne?

She leaned back in the chair and closed her eyes, uncertain of what came next and terrified how much she cared.

OLIVIA FLOATED somewhere between sleep and wakefulness.

The squeak of shoe soles on the slick white tiles of the floor dragged her awake. She raised her head, getting her bearings in the dimly lit room.

A nurse stood next to Jack's IV pump, raised a bottle, shoved a needle into it and pulled down the plunger. The syringe filled with clear liquid and the nurse put the bottle down on the edge of the bed next to Jack.

"What is that?" She cleared her throat.

The nurse stared unseeing in her direction and inserted the syringe's needle into the IV line.

"Wait. What are you giving him?" Caution rattled through her.

She stood up, stepped around the end of the bed and came face to face with the unresponsive nurse.

"What did you give him?"

The discarded bottle lay on the bed. She reached for it at the same time as the nurse. Getting to it just before she did.

Potassium chloride.

Terror gelled in her veins.

She'd done a story on the drug used in lethal injections to stop the heart.

The nurse had just given Jack a megadose of the deadly liquid.

Olivia grabbed the IV tube where it was attached to the needle going into Jack's arm and yanked it out.

The IV pump went into alarm mode.

High-pitched beeping raked over her nerves.

The annoying sound becoming louder as she pressed the call button.

Jack jolted awake and sat up. He stared down at the blood streaming from his arm where his IV had been attached.

A nurse stood at the end of his bed, her mouth agape in horror.

"Olivia?" He made eye contact with her, noting her look of relief.

"She just tried to kill you with potassium chloride."

"I...I'd never do that." The nurse shook her head violently. "That's a strictly controlled drug. It wasn't prescribed for Mr. Trayborne."

The room filled with medical staff, all trying to assess the situation.

Doctor Perkins stepped into the room and the sea of nurses parted. "What's going on?"

One of the nurses reached into her pocket and pulled out a packet of gauze.

Jack stretched out his right arm for her to clean and bandage the IV site.

He pulled in a deep breath and found peace in the chaos around him. Olivia stood to the left of his bed. He reached out, taking her hand. He squeezed and she squeezed back. She'd just saved his life. She'd been paying attention, been true to her vow to protect him. But what had caused the nurse to inject the lethal drug in the first place? Telepathic manipulation? No place felt safe.

"It was nothing, Doctor Perkins. A simple mistake." Jack let loose of Olivia's hand, pulled back the covers and climbed out of bed. "I'd like you to sign my release form."

I can better defend myself at home, was a more precise thought, but he kept that fact to himself. He suspected the man in the ski mask who'd put him here in the first place was behind the nurse's mistake. She'd simply been his weapon of choice.

A jolt of caution burned through him as he stared at the individuals in the room. Any one of them could be utilized at anytime. A fact that left him little choice.

"I'd like to recover at home. Miss Morgan," he met her eye to eye, "will take excellent care of me. Make sure I'm okay."

Jack swallowed, looking at her just long enough to feel the rage of desire flare in his veins.

"If you don't mind, I'd like to get dressed now."

One by one, they left the cramped hospital room, but Jack could hear the nurse being redressed in the hallway outside by Doctor Perkins.

"It wasn't her fault." He took his clothes out of the closet while Olivia closed the door. "Her actions were manipulated telepathically."

Olivia turned back around, stopped in her tracks by the sight of Jack standing next to the bed in his birthday suit, body all taut, hard muscle and smooth skin. Power and tenderness, intertwined.

An ache took hold inside of her, sending flames of desire sizzling along every nerve ending in her body, until she was sure she could hear the sound of blazing lust in her eardrums.

"We're not safe here, or anywhere for that matter." He pulled on his pants. "I want you to exercise extreme caution…" He stared back at her. "Olivia? Are you hearing me?"

"No." She moved around the end of the bed and into his arms. What was happening between them? She needed to know. Needed to understand why being with him turned her insides to jelly. Gave her the sensation of being…cared for?

He stepped back from her, reached down and caught

her chin. Raising her face, he stared down at her, a half smile on his mouth. Did he feel it, too?

She gazed into his eyes. Their color deepened, before the smile faded.

His eyes narrowed. "I liked it, too. Hell, I more than liked it and I'd be happy to demonstrate the other techniques I have at my disposal, but you must snap out of it. Things are becoming progressively more dangerous and I don't want to lose you. Where's that savvy, smart-mouthed woman who puts frustration in my veins?"

"You're right." *He was right.* Her blood cooled and she stepped around the end of the bed, opening a mental and physical space between them, but anticipation lingered in her cells long after contact was broken.

Jack gritted his teeth and pulled on his shirt. Holding her in his arms had eroded more of his resistance to the mysterious emotion sluicing in his veins and making him fuzzy-headed. Before too much longer, holding her would be all he wanted to do, a fact that did little to ease the worry riding his thoughts. He needed Olivia to keep thinking, to be a participant in her own security. He could protect her, but not without her vigilance.

The man in the ski mask was growing stronger, becoming bolder with every attempt he made on their lives. But who was he and what did he want?

Buttoning the last button on his shirt, he put on his socks and shoes, snagged Olivia's hand and headed for the exit. He needed time to think, time to dissect the circumstances surrounding them.

He pulled open the heavy door and they stepped into the hallway.

At the north end of the corridor was the nurse's station. He needed to make sure the nurse who'd tried to inject him with potassium chloride, didn't lose her job over an incident that was beyond her control. However, he didn't plan to tell Doctor Perkins just how far beyond her control it had really been. Part of what made the Phantom work in Black's Cove was his anonymity.

"Look, it's Judy Bartholomew's room." Olivia took a hesitant right into room 360, spotting Judy's husband holding baby Gracie.

Jack followed her in.

"Judy?" Olivia whispered, seeing the young mother sitting up in her hospital bed, looking as good as the day she'd first met her on Main Street and asked her about Jack Trayborne.

Olivia's heart rebounded. She'd been so worried the young woman wouldn't survive, wouldn't be around to raise her sweet little girl.

"Yes." She stared at Olivia, no sign of recognition on her face, but the moment she spotted Jack, a smile spread on her mouth. "Mr. Trayborne. It's nice to see you again. What are you doing here?"

"I heard you were here. I happened to be here myself, so I thought I'd stop and see how you're doing."

"Much better, I believe, at least that's what they tell me." She glanced over at her husband and baby, then back at Jack. "Thank you for coming by."

"You're welcome." Jack grasped Olivia's hand and led her back out into the hallway. Judy's husband followed.

"I'm sorry she doesn't remember you, Miss Morgan. But the coma erased her short-term memory."

"Do you know why she took those pills?"

Mr. Bartholomew shifted under the question, his dismay imprinted on his young face in the form of confusion that pulled his eyebrows together and grouped his features in a tight formation. "*She* can't even remember taking them…." His voice broke and he looked down at Gracie. "I didn't even know there was a problem."

Olivia reached out and squeezed his arm. "I'm sorry. I wish there was something I could do."

Grace pawed at her with one tiny hand and she caught the baby girl's fingers. "It will work out. She has so much to live for."

"You're right." Mr. Bartholomew nodded. "The psychologist has been in several times…. We're going to get through this. Thank you both for your concern."

Her heart ached for him as he turned back into the room and Jack took her hand.

"I'm so glad she pulled through."

Jack laced his fingers in Olivia's and steered her down the corridor, his suspicions little more than a niggling at the moment, but bound to take a track straight to the man in the ski mask who had the power to manipulate using telepathic suggestion. Was he behind Judy's near-death experience?

Tension twisted the muscles tight between his shoulder blades. Judy had given up the information about where to find the estate. He'd always believed that Diana and Rick had something to do with Judy's accident, but now he wasn't so sure.

The double glass doors at the end of the corridor near the ER slid open.

A deputy raced into the hospital with his arm around the shoulder of another officer.

"Help! Can we get some help? My partner has cobra venom in his eyes. He can't see."

Jack's heart rate shot up and he sprinted to where Officer Mel Roberts stood with his injured partner.

A nurse rushed forward and led the officer to an exam room.

"The missing cobra from Diana's shop?" Jack asked, pausing next to the upset officer who leaned forward, putting his hands on his knees.

"Yeah. We cornered it in the alley behind the shop and called animal control, but the damn thing put up one hell of a fight."

"Where is it now?"

"Not sure. It wiggled into a crack between the two buildings. I'm afraid we can't get to it in there." The officer straightened.

"You know Diana's operation. Maybe you can wrangle him out?"

Jack hesitated, mostly because Olivia was squeezing his hand so hard it hurt.

He did know the operation, he'd set it up to help the

Foundation and Diana. He had an obligation to capture the dangerous cobra before anyone else got hurt.

"I'll head over there right now."

Chapter Eleven

"When did you become a deadly snake wrangler?"

"When I set Diana up with her milking operation five years ago, so she could supply the Trayborne Foundation Research Labs in Atlanta and Los Angeles with the venom."

Olivia's muscles tensed. Venomous snakes, laboratory research, they were diametrically opposed to one another.

"The research is promising, Olivia. It could one day annihilate the world's most deadly viruses."

"Please avoid my thoughts, Jack. You know no matter what you say, I hate snakes."

"Yes, I do know that." He took her hand, maneuvering her out the back door of the pet shop and into the dark alley.

Jack heightened his senses. "Grab that trash can and put it down over there," he motioned to a spot next to the door, "and go back inside if you like."

He listened to her heart rate slow, heard her pull

several tentative breaths deep into her lungs. He was glad she was going to stay. He couldn't lose sight of her, not even for a moment.

Combing the darkness with his vision, he closed in on the snakes' location, nestled in the three-inch crack separating the ancient brick buildings from each other.

"I found him."

She mentally shuddered, probably physically too, but he wiped the image of her smooth skin excited with a chill from his mind and trained his focus on his prey.

He'd soothe her later, after the cobra was back in its cage where it couldn't endanger the residents of Black's Cove again.

How had the snake gotten past Diana's defenses? he wondered as he stepped closer, picking up the reptile's scent trail. He must be close, no more than six feet away.

Was it possible she'd been a victim of the same man who wanted both of them dead?

Caution rode his nerves, saddled by the knowledge that something Diana understood fully had killed her completely.

Another bait situation? A way to draw him out, like he'd drawn Olivia out, using Diana, and right into the path of an oncoming train?

Movement near the head of the alley distracted Jack's attention.

The cobra streaked from the narrow crack and became airborne.

Instinct took over. Jack trained a beam of energy on the snake, coming in contact with the beam guiding it.

The snake disintegrated in midair.

Jack refocused, surrounding Olivia in a protective shield.

He turned to find the masked man standing in the alley less than a hundred feet away.

"You can't save her every time, Jack." He stepped forward. "You can do only one thing at a time." He reached out and raised the Dumpster twenty feet in the air.

Caution hissed through Jack as he watched the one-ton bin move to within ten feet of where he stood.

"What's it going to be, Jack? Self-preservation or her life? You can't have both."

Anger ignited in his veins, rage and hostility, tempered by his sense of right. He could do only one thing at a time, a fact that was becoming abundantly clear to their tormenter. His Achilles' heel.

If he released Olivia to protect himself, the thug would snatch her before he had the chance to recover.

He reached for the man's thoughts and found a wall.

"You can't get in!"

"What do you want?"

"You know what I want. Think, Jack."

He lunged left, released the energy bubble surrounding Olivia and sent a burst out, catching the masked thug off guard.

The pulse hit him full on, knocking him backward and into the street.

Jack dodged the Dumpster as it hit the ground inches from his head and folded up like a tin can.

A car horn blared.

He jumped to his feet and raced to the head of the alley, but the man in the mask was nowhere to be seen.

Turning, he found Olivia standing next to him, her face stark white in the glare of the street lamp overhead.

Reaching for her, he pulled her into his arms. "It's okay. He's gone."

"It's not okay. It'll never be okay until we know who he is and what he wants."

Holding her against him, he knew she was right, and he knew where they had to start.

OLIVIA SHOVED the last medical file across the table to Jack and leaned back in her chair. They'd been at it for hours, sifting through the files on the test subjects in Doctor Trayborne's experiment. She now officially knew every detail about the program.

"I give up. There's nothing that indicates any of you developed the ability for telepathic manipulation, but some of the other stuff is, well…out there."

Jack smiled and leaned forward, putting his elbows on the table. "You should have witnessed my early years, learning to control and grow my abilities."

"You mean they weren't finite after the initial treatment?"

"No. Each one of us developed at different rates. My powers didn't become fixed until I was in my late teens."

Excitement buzzed along her nerves and she sat forward. "So any one of you could have developed the ability to telepathically manipulate well after your grandfather stopped monitoring each subject?"

"Yes, but the terms of the trust are explicit. Any and all abilities or changes are to be disclosed in order for the money to be released."

"And you believed they'd step forward and reveal everything?"

Jack's face was so serious that she couldn't hold in the laugh that rattled up her throat.

"They're not to be trusted, Jack. Just because they denied developing new abilities doesn't mean they didn't. Did your grandfather physically examine any of them?"

"Yes, but only up until the age of 18. After that they filled out a yearly profile. There's another problem, Olivia. Four of them are dead." He slid a red folder across the table to her.

"How?"

"Joseph Sabato died in a fire two years ago. His autopsy and death certificate are in there. We know firsthand that Diana is dead. Sam Campbell flew his airplane into the Pacific sunset. They found the wreckage floating in the ocean, but no body. The authorities suspected suicide, but he didn't leave a note. That was five years ago." Jack rubbed his hands up and down his face several times, and leaned across the table.

"I think it's weird," Olivia said, reaching for the file and flipping it open, "considering what happened to Judy Bartholomew, and that nurse trying to inject you with potassium chloride. Maybe someone used telepathic manipulation on them. What happened to the last one?"

"She drove her car off a cliff." Jack stared at her,

letting her observation sink in. Why hadn't he seen it before? Had the other test subjects been picked off one by one, drawing a path straight back to Black's Cove? Dread crept through his body, coating his nerves in mind-numbing caution. Who was next?

Olivia grabbed two of the files and shoved them toward him. "There are only two who have a chance of being behind this. Rick Dowdy and my brother. But we both know Ross is stuck in a wheelchair in a Phoenix care center a thousand miles from here. That leaves Mr. Dowdy."

"What are the chances someone else got hold of the formula?"

"Doubtful. It's been entombed in the vault since my grandfather realized how dangerous it could be if it fell into the wrong hands."

"Does anyone else have access?"

"No. I'm the only one."

Jack glanced at the two files, then back up at her. "I've had enough of this for one night."

Olivia smiled, her soft full lips turning up at the corners and driving his mind in several wild directions at the same time. Desire flared, burning unchecked in his veins. He pushed back his chair and stood up. Wanting her. Needing her. Those were emotions foreign to him only a month ago, but now he found himself drawn to the language they spoke inside of him. Answering in the only way he knew how. By touching her.

He reached out and took her hand, pulling her to her

feet. "In the morning, we'll drive into Black's Cove and talk to Rick Dowdy."

Olivia leaned into him, feeling safe as he wrapped his arms around her and held her close. Was there even a chance that Ross was somehow involved? She doubted it, considering the extent of his brain damage. He was forever chained to a wheelchair, of that she was certain.

"What do you say we take it upstairs?" he asked, holding her away from him, but not too far.

She instantly missed the contact of his body pressed to hers. Its warmth, the way it made pleasant sensations dance over her skin wherever he touched her.

"I'd like that."

OLIVIA DRAGGED HER EYES open and found her bearings in the dark room. She glanced at the clock on the night-stand—3:00 a.m. Sliding her foot across the silky sheet, she searched for Jack beside her, but he wasn't there.

She rolled over, catching sight of him standing at the massive window on the south side of the room, his naked body silhouetted against the filmy sheers he held open.

"Jack," she whispered.

He didn't move.

"What is it?" Caution caught her nerves in its grasp and she climbed out of bed, moving toward him, her feet silent on the thick carpet.

He reached for her and pulled her against him. "Do you see that?"

Straining to see something in the far-reaching landscape outside, she finally focused in the direction of the clinic.

"There's a tiny light on, in the northeast corner. Do you see it?"

The faintest flicker caught and held her attention, like a small star in the sky, there and not there. "Sort of. What is it? The power is off because of the fire isn't it? Is there a backup generator?"

"No."

He brushed his hand down her bare back, exciting every nerve ending in her body. She moaned in delight. Making love with him had taken her beyond ecstacy, to a level she'd never experienced in her life. She wasn't sure she could ever go back. She didn't want to.

"I have to investigate, Olivia."

Fear intertwined with caution inside of her and she grasped his forearm, hanging on to him. "I'm going with you."

Jack could feel her shaking, the message telegraphed through her hand where it locked onto his arm. He'd give anything to pick her up, carry her back to his bed and make love to her until dawn, but he couldn't let the light go this time. He'd seen it once before, two weeks ago, and put it off as an emergency lamp running on a battery source until he found all the batteries were dead.

Someone haunted the clinic. He was determined to find out who. Tonight. With Olivia in tow? He cared more about her than he'd ever imagined was possible, but would she be safe here, unprotected from a madman with skills that rivaled his own?

"Get dressed, wear your tennis shoes. We're going cross-country."

OLIVIA TRIED TO RELAX as Jack maneuvered them along a narrow path through the woods. The chill of the October night air wreaked havoc on her body's thermostat. But she couldn't blame it all on the temperature. Her stomach was in knots, her nerves as frayed as the bottom hem on a pair of cutoff jeans. Jack was the only thing holding her together.

Staring past him, she focused on the light to keep from turning tail. The man who wanted them dead was cunning. He'd somehow managed to almost get past Jack's defenses time and again and if anything happened to Jack...well, she'd...she couldn't live with the thought. She was falling for him. Hard.

Jack slowed and pulled her with him into a stand of aspens. "It's still on." His voice was whisper quiet and she watched him straighten and pull in a deep breath of air.

"What are you doing?"

"I have heightened senses whenever I employ them. I see clearly in the dark. Sometimes I can smell the enemy, depending on the direction of the wind. And I can hear the slightest sound of movement. That's how I detected the bomb in your car."

"And what about touch."

He trailed his fingertips along her jawline and lowered his mouth to hers.

The kiss took her breath away and left her winded when he pulled back.

"All-consuming," he whispered against her ear.

Olivia heated in sync with the primal need exploding between them, forcing them together like magnets.

She was in over-the-top, howl-at-the-moon, got-to-have-him lust, with Jack Trayborne.

Damn. She pulled the thought back, praying he hadn't entered her head space and tagged it.

"Are we going in the front?" she asked, fixing her stare on the light shining through the window of the room in the corner of the clinic where she'd climbed the fire escape both times she'd broken in.

"There's a service entrance on the northwest corner. We'll enter there and work our way upstairs."

Dread washed over her and she couldn't paddle her way out of it. The thought of entering the building, where she'd almost been cooked, made her jittery.

"It'll be okay, Olivia. I won't let anything happen to you." He squeezed her hand and some of her worry evaporated.

Jack stepped from behind the trees holding on to her. So far, he hadn't detected anything out of the ordinary and apart from the light, there was no indication that anyone lurked nearby. Still, agitation rubbed over his nerves and put his senses on alert.

They reached the service door. Jack dug the key out of his pocket and used it to open the door. He paused, pulling information from their surroundings.

The night was still, calm, the first wisps of mist were

just beginning to creep up from the earth and spread out over the grounds. A preamble to dawn at Black's Cove that had been transpiring for centuries.

He focused his attention on the interior of the building, picking up the sound of a low hum coming from somewhere inside.

Caution bit and held on to his nerves. He stepped through the entrance and took hold of Olivia's hand.

The strong smell of smoke hung in the air, a result of the charred walls they brushed past as they moved down a narrow corridor and out into the massive dining hall.

Jack scanned the darkness and came up empty.

He pulled Olivia to the stairs, scanning the length of them before they started up. At the landing, he paused again.

The hum was growing louder. Whatever it was, it was on this floor.

Scanning left, he saw a narrow beam of light shining from underneath the door at the end of the hallway, but the hum was coming from the opposite end.

Caution pulsed inside of him. Which way? The light represented the most risk. Someone had turned it on. And someone could still be inside the room.

He moved left, focusing his senses completely on the strip of light.

They reached the door and he pushed it open, prepared to take on whoever was inside, but the place was empty except for an LED light sitting on the window sill.

Jack stepped inside, seeing a trail of footprints in the layer of dust on the floor.

Two sets of tracks. Two people had recently been in the room, but what were they doing here?

"Jack, look at this."

He turned in time to see her step toward the opposite corner of the room.

"It's my laptop!"

"Don't touch—" Before the warning was off his tongue, Olivia bent down and picked up the computer.

Jack felt the vibration of the explosion under his feet.

The floor shifted.

Reaching out he pulled her to him, wrapped his arms around her and encased them in a protective shield.

Falling, they were falling.

The floor fell away, sending them crashing down into the basement thirty feet below.

They hit bottom.

The impact jarred Jack's bones, but he maintained his grip on Olivia.

Tons of debris rained down on them, impacting the shield and burying them alive beneath it.

Olivia's heart pounded so loud that he could hear it without trying. "Relax, we're going to be fine." He brushed his hand against her hair, feeling her terror ease.

Seconds later, the last piece of debris rained down and the air stilled.

"What happened?"

"The laptop was booby-trapped. Picking it up set off a charge that blew out the floor from underneath us." Worry sliced into him as he stared up at the mess piled on top of them.

He was immediately thankful for the impenetrable darkness that prevented Olivia from seeing the inside of their tomb. If he released the bubble to clear it away, they'd be crushed. If he did nothing, they would die.

Searching in the darkness, he spotted a measure of hope rising up out of the chaos, a main support pillar less than three feet to their right. If they could reach it and take cover behind it, he could release the bubble and let the debris settle into the void, making it possible for them to climb out.

It was a risky plan, but it was the only chance they had.

He let go of her and stood up. "We've got to push three feet to the right. There's a support column there."

"Can't you just sweep this stuff away?"

"No. If I release the shield, the debris will bury us."

She was silent in the darkness. He heard her sharp intake of breath, felt the invasive tension charge the air around them.

"You can only do one thing at a time?"

"Yes." The admission pulled his nerves taut and made him feel inadequate. "It seems our tormenter has mastered what I haven't. The ability to manipulate more than one object simultaneously."

"He can juggle a couple of things at once. So what?" She stood up next to him. "He can't read your mind or he would have known what you planned to do in the alley and after the car accident. He's good, Jack, but you're better." She reached for him and he escaped into the feel of her body against his. All these years, his skills had gone unchallenged. He wouldn't cower at the first sign of resistance.

"Push," he said, grasping her hands in the dark and placing them on the shell of the shield. "We can manipulate this energy field until we get to the column."

Olivia tried to understand the texture of the bubble encasing her and saving her from becoming a human pancake. The skin was tough under her hands, but it also gave with the pressure and she felt the entire mass move forward a couple of inches.

"Good. Again."

Another laborious shove. More movement.

"I wish I could see where we were going."

"No, I don't think you do."

She smiled in the darkness, thankful he was beside her. Without him, she'd have died in the fire that created the hole they found themselves in now. Without him, the newfound emotion coursing in her veins wouldn't exist.

"Good." Jack reached through the barrier and smacked the pillar with his fist, making sure it was intact. Structurally, the building was sound, at least that was the engineer's take on it after the fire had gutted the basement. Still, he planned to have it razed in the spring.

"It's risky, Olivia." Jack reached for her and lowered his mouth to hers, melding them together in the silent darkness. He pulled back, struck by something that hadn't fully registered in his head until this moment.

He more than cared for her…

"The instant I release the shield, take cover behind the pillar. The debris is going to settle. I'll hold it back, but whatever you do, stay put."

"I'm ready." Fear ground across her nerves. It would help if she could see. At least she'd know what was coming.

Jack took her hand. She gripped his back so hard that her fingers tingled, but hanging on to him was her only tangible hope at the moment. Trust worked its way through her and settled in her head. She did trust Jack. With her life. But with her heart?

He yanked her forward, catching her off guard.

The ground under her feet shifted. She sucked in a mouthful of dust.

"Grab hold," Jack yelled as small bits of debris rained down on her in the dark.

He pulled her left, then back to the right, putting her hand in contact with a massive column she estimated to be at least three feet around.

"Hang on." Jack splayed his body over hers, covering her, protecting her.

Olivia closed her eyes, trying to stay calm as boards clattered around them and splintered against the solid pillar.

She choked on the thick air. Reaching down, she pulled the neck of her T-shirt up over her nose and mouth to filter out some of the dust.

"Olivia?" he said against her ear. "Are you okay?"

Squeezing her eyes open, she was shocked to see a

dim blanket of light covering the opening straight up and to the left of them. Dawn was breaking.

"Yeah, I need a bath and some fresh air, but I'm fine."

Jack let go of her, stepped back and stared up at the jagged hole in what was once the basement ceiling. A waist-high pile of debris lay in front of them and had streamed out on both sides of the pillar. They were trapped against a concrete wall. The only way out was up.

"Do you want to fly?" he asked her, watching her mouth bow up into a grin from under a layer of grime. She could be covered in mud for all he cared, but he'd still believe she was the most beautiful woman he'd ever seen.

"You're going to toss me up there?" She nodded to the gaping hole.

"Yes."

"How are you going to get out? Can you fly?"

"No. I can manipulate you, but I have to do it the old-fashioned way, climb."

"There used to be a ladder in the kitchen. I had to move it to get down into the file room. If it's still there you could use it to get out."

"Okay. Are you ready?"

"Yeah."

Reaching out, Jack lifted her up just above the debris field. The clearance was tight.

"Pull up your legs."

She immediately did as he asked and he pushed her through the opening in a beam of energy, hearing her feet touch the ground overhead.

"Are you clear?"

"Yeah. I'm going for the ladder."

Jack heightened his senses, tuning into her hesitant footsteps against the hardwood floor. Her heart rate was escalating, her breath coming in ragged gasps. What was going on? Why was she so frightened?

Olivia screamed. Her voice high-pitched and terrified. Razors of worry sliced across his nerves.

He lunged for the debris pile, pawing over shattered boards, chunks of plaster and concrete.

OLIVIA STOOD AS STILL as she could, the blade of a knife pressed to her throat, its edge biting into her skin, just enough to cut her. Blood trickled down her neck in tiny rivulets she couldn't brush away.

Had he lost his mind? Or was he a victim of telepathic manipulation? Being forced into doing something he wouldn't normally do?

"Stop, Stuart," she pleaded, "you're hurting me."

"You have to die." The unnatural cadence of his voice rocked her to the core.

Where was Jack?

"Please let me go. Jack needs help."

No response.

The pressure on the knife increased.

Terror burned through her.

Stuart Redmond was going to kill her.

Chapter Twelve

Jack cleared the jagged opening and crawled out, the cuts on his hands and arms leaving a trail of blood on the dirty floor.

Pulling in information from around him, he came to his feet.

Olivia's scream had come from near the kitchen. He sucked up next to the wall, easing down the narrow hallway on its path to the dining room.

Light infiltrated the building through broken windows and soot-covered panes.

He reached the end of the hall and glanced around the corner, catching sight of Olivia being held at knife point by…Stuart?

Caution locked into step with his anger. Reaching out, he grabbed the knife in a beam of energy and flung it across the room.

Stuart immediately released Olivia and fell back.

Jack rushed across the room. "Are you okay?"

"Yeah. It's superficial." She brushed at her neck.

He turned his attention to Stuart, who sat on the floor, looking dazed and confused.

"Stuart?" Jack knelt next to the man who'd been caring for his family for over thirty years. Reaching out, he shook Stuart's shoulder.

"Where…where am I?" Stuart looked up at him, recognition passing over his features like a cloud passes over the sun. "Sir? Oh dear, what have I done?"

Jack helped him to his feet and turned his attention back to Olivia. The knife marks on her neck were tiny, but when he thought of how close he'd just come to losing her…

"How'd you get here, Stuart?"

"I don't know."

"Let's go home."

"Very well, sir." Stuart turned for the main door and Jack took Olivia's hand, following him to the exit.

He stared at Stuart's shoe prints in the dust on the floor. Caution invaded his thoughts and drove him to an odd conclusion. Stuart's prints were remarkably similar in size and shape to the ones he'd seen near the light in the room upstairs. Had he been manipulated to do that as well? It was certainly possible.

Foreboding attached itself to his outlook. Anyone at anytime could be used as a weapon against them. People they loved and cared about. Vigilant, he had to remain vigilant.

Outside, the air was shrouded in mist, obscuring the landscape around the clinic. Stuart's pickup sat in the driveway just outside the gatehouse.

Jack scanned the fog, coming up empty. Nobody else was out there.

Uneasiness churned through him like a tidal wave. Was it possible Stuart was still acting under telepathic manipulation? If so, was Olivia still in danger?

"I'll drive."

Stuart dragged the keys out of his pocket and handed them to him.

Jack studied his face. He seemed like he was back to normal, but he reached for Stuart's thoughts to alleviate his concern.

"I'll have eggs for breakfast. And some bacon. I really like Muriel's cornbread muffins. I think I'll have a couple of those…."

Jack pulled back, satisfied the control over Stuart had run its course.

They climbed into the pickup and Jack fired the engine. Glancing in the rearview mirror, he scanned the fog, watching the last vestiges of the clinic disappear in its icy hand.

Maybe he shouldn't wait until spring to demolish it. Maybe he should do it now.

OLIVIA PUT THE morning paper down on the table and picked up her cup of coffee. Raising her gaze, she found Jack staring at her.

His look of longing spoke to her on a visceral level and she could no longer deny that she loved him, but her days in Black's Cove were numbered. She was a journalist. She needed another story, like a junkie needed another fix, and she could never betray the trust he'd given her by telling his secret to the world.

"When do you plan to stop running, Olivia?"

The question caught her off guard, but it was useless to try and maneuver her way out of it; he'd simply reach into her mind and read it for himself.

"Ya caught me with my racing shoes on, didn't ya?"

"Sometimes you have to stand and fight. Face the guilt and resentment you feel toward Ross and your parents for the lack of a normal childhood and beat it down. Relegate it to the past and move on. You can never get back those years and those relationships. Acceptance could go a long way toward healing."

He was right, dammit. Tears stung the back of her eyes and she swallowed hard.

"Let the chips fall where they may and stay out from under them?" The answer sounded so easy in her own words.

"Yes. That's all you have to do. That's all you've ever had to do." He stood up, reached for her and pulled her up into his arms.

She buried her face against his broad chest, feeling a ten-ton weight lift off her. Maybe she was a little like Dorothy with the ruby slippers; she'd always had the capability to go home, but not the know-how to get there.

"You could have a life…here, with me."

She pulled back, staring up into his handsome face. A face she'd come to love, on a man she'd come to need more than the air in the room. She opened her mouth, but nothing came out.

"Don't give me an answer now. Stay until I find and stop the madman who wants to rip you away from me forever."

He pulled out her chair for her and released her into it. She sat back down feeling dazed. Could she make a life with Jack?

Reaching up she touched the spot on her neck where he'd dressed her knife wound. Not if their unknown tormenter had his way.

"Tell me about Stuart. What's his relationship to your family?"

"He's been here since I was born. He has a son, Benton, three years older than me. We used to play together as kids, until he went away to boarding school. Stuart's late-wife, Mildred, was my grandfather's lab assistant. She went through all of the research, development and disbursements of NPQ."

"Where is she now?"

"She died ten years ago, just weeks after my grandfather passed away. She nursed him through his illness. He provided quite nicely for her, and Stuart in his will. Unfortunately, she didn't live to enjoy any of it."

"That's dedication." *Or was it more than that?* she wondered as she picked up the mug of coffee and raised it to her lips. Sometimes the answers were right under your nose.

The shuffle of footsteps racing down the hallway pulled her out of contemplation.

"Sir!" Frances burst into the room, her cheeks flushed, her breath coming in gasps. "Your hotel, sir. It's on fire!"

JACK STARED AT the billowing funnel of black smoke twisting up from the horizon and pressed the accelerator to the floor. The Mercedes picked up speed.

The hotel was filled to capacity with a convention of grain growers. Lives were at stake.

"Take it easy, Jack! The hotel has smoke alarms and a sprinkler system. I'm sure everyone is safe."

Olivia's attempts to reassure him helped, but he couldn't shake the sound of the thug's threats from his brain. Had this fire been set intentionally to hurt him, to hurt people he cared about?

He slowed the car and made the corner into town, thumping over the train tracks and whizzing down backstreets until he pulled into the parking lot of the hotel, slammed on the brakes and came to a stop.

Horror laced through his bloodstream, constricting every vessel in his body. The parking lot was full of patrons, milling around in various states of dress.

The south side of the fourth floor was fully involved. Flames licked out of window openings, reaching for the fifth floor in their ravenous appetite for fuel.

Smoke spewed from the windows on the fifth floor. It was only a matter of time before the fire broke through.

Jack climbed out of the car and raced for the fire chief, Fred Baxter, standing next to the command vehicle.

The searing heat almost pushed him back, but he remained focused.

"Fred!" Jack yelled over the drone of the pumps.

The chief looked up, spotted him and strode forward.

"Hell of a blaze, Jack. Called in around 5:00 a.m. We're beating it down, but it's stubborn."

"Did everyone make it out?"

Fred's features dropped, leaving Jack with only one answer. Anger sluiced in his veins and he stepped closer.

"How many, Fred?"

"One couple from the fourth floor is unaccounted for. Everyone else made it out alive."

Jack stared at the blazing building, growing more dangerous with each passing second.

He had to go in. He had to find them. He took several steps forward.

"No, Jack! You can't do it. It's too dangerous. The fire could flash over anytime!" Fred grabbed his arm.

Horror stilled him, turning to resolve in his veins as he stared up at the roof, catching sight of flailing arms through the intense smoke.

"Where's the ladder truck?"

"Ours is too short. We've got the mutual aid structure truck coming in from Soda Springs."

Raising his finger, he pointed at the far northeast corner of the roof, where the missing couple waved frantically.

Hope surged in his veins. He turned back toward the car where he'd left Olivia. The passenger door was open; the car was empty. He looked for her in the crowd who'd exited the fire and spotted the top of her head.

She'd be doing what she did best. Asking questions.

He had to rescue the couple before the roof gave way or the acrid smoke asphyxiated them.

Pulling back, he turned and raced for a grove of trees

on the perimeter of the parking lot. He needed cover to work, to protect the Phantom's anonymity.

HE WAS CRAZY, nuts, deranged. Olivia fought the man who'd pulled her out of the crowd and was now dragging her through the hotel lobby.

"Who are you? What are you doing?"

He stopped, pulled open the stairwell door at the back of the burning building and shoved her inside.

"Go to the roof," he demanded.

Fear slammed into her brain. Resist.

She whirled on him. "No!" Lunging at him, she ducked under his arm and aimed for the exit door in her desperate attempt to escape.

Olivia yanked on the handle, but the door wouldn't open.

"Go to the roof." His dark eyes narrowed.

She shook her head. "We have to get out of here."

Slowly, he extended his good hand; the other was in a sling. She felt her feet leave the ground. Staring at him in horror, she tried to understand who he was.

He manipulated her toward the stairs, pushing her up them with the same power Jack possessed. "Jack's here! He won't let you hurt me."

No response.

She tried to shake loose, but it was like being a fly stuck in a spider's web.

Panic ignited in her veins as they moved past the fourth-floor door. She could feel the heat radiating from the other side. What was he doing? She had to talk some sense into him because she certainly couldn't over-power him.

"My name is Olivia Morgan. I'm a journalist." Nothing. There was something familiar about him. The hospital, he was the man who'd come in with a shoulder injury the morning they brought in Judy Bartholomew. He was Rick Dowdy.

"You're hurting me, Rick."

For an instant, he looked at her and she almost thought she saw recognition in his eyes. This was the man Jack suspected had something to do with the attempts on her life. The man they'd planned to speak with this morning after breakfast.

"Rick!" she yelled, desperate to get through to him.

They passed the landing marked by a large 5 above the exit. Smoke seeped through the crack under the door and burned her eyes as it filled the stairwell above them.

"The hotel's on fire! We've got to get out!"

They reached the sixth-floor landing and he dropped her. Olivia scrambled to her feet.

He pulled open the door and shoved her out onto the roof.

JACK SURROUNDED the couple together in a bubble of protection, raised them up over the edge of the roof and lowered them safely to the ground from his hiding place in the trees.

Relief washed over him as he pulled back, taking one more look at the burning hotel.

His breath caught. His throat closed.

Heightening his senses, he focused on a man and woman moving precariously close to the edge of the roof.

On the ground below, a collective intake of breath whispered over the airwaves and ground in his ears.

Rick Dowdy…and Olivia.

Caution tempered his first response, to jettison Dowdy from the roof and slam him to earth where he'd never be able to touch her again.

He reached for the man's thoughts instead, finding them easily in the chaos swirling in his head.

Kill her…she has to die…push her. Telepathic manipulation? Or the conscious rambling of a madman?

Dowdy lunged forward, shoving Olivia.

She went airborne, off the roof.

Her shriek of terror glanced off Jack's eardrums.

Reaching out he caught her three stories from the asphalt below.

Time to die.

He picked up Dowdy's thought, but it was too late. In a sickening second, Rick Dowdy plunged off the building before Jack could get Olivia to the ground.

Jack closed his eyes for a second before he manipulated her away from the horrific scene and put her down near a squad car where an officer rushed to her side.

Why had he done it? Committed suicide…and he'd tried to take Olivia with him.

Jack's gut fisted. Was it possible Dowdy was behind everything? Did he have abilities that went unreported? Or was he a victim along with the others? Now they would never get the chance to find out.

He stepped out from behind the trees and headed for Olivia, who had quite unceremoniously collapsed on the ground in shock the moment he'd released her.

JACK PULLED THE Mercedes into the garage, unable to shake the uneasiness spreading through him like wildfire.

Where was Stuart? He'd always been there to offer his assistance when he arrived home.

"Something is wrong," he said in a low voice, glancing at Olivia in the seat next to him. "Stuart isn't here. Let's go inside quietly."

Her blue eyes went wide. He could hear her heartbeat amp up. She'd had more than enough excitement for one day and he wanted nothing more than to take her in his arms and help her forget.

She nodded and reached for the door handle. Together, they climbed out of the car and eased the doors closed. The pop of the latches closing echoed in the cavernous garage.

Olivia felt another tremor of fear rise in her body and rattle her bones, but it abated when she picked up the tire iron off the workbench. Jack had his defenses, but she was sorely without his abilities.

An amused grin pulled on his mouth, just before she hunkered down behind him for the trip into the house.

Jack opened the service entrance into the kitchen and stepped inside with Olivia behind him. He heightened his senses, taking in information from around him. Normally, Muriel would be preparing dinner at this time of the afternoon. His gaze traveled to the chopping block where a pile of carrots lay untouched.

Reaching back, he grasped Olivia's hand and pointed at the chopping block. He closed his eyes, focusing his hearing.

Thump…thump. A pause. Thump…thump. A rhythm, like the sound of a fist against a wall. Hollow…desperate.

"Come on." He pulled Olivia through the kitchen and out into the service hallway. Stopping next to the closet, the hidden entrance down into the lab, he pulled open the door.

Empty, but the coats had been pushed aside on the rod in both directions, exposing the switch that engaged the elevator. Caution hissed through him. Had the lab been breached?

Thump…thump. Pause. Thump…thump.

He honed in on the sound. It was coming from upstairs.

Jack headed for the stairs. Letting go of Olivia's hand, he took the stairs two at a time.

Rushing down the hall, he stopped and yanked on the closet door, but it was locked. He turned the skeleton key and the door shot open.

Muriel and Frances burst out and sprawled on the floor. Their feet and hands were tied, a gag shoved in each of their mouths.

Jack stared into the back of the closet spotting Stuart sitting upright against the wall.

"Oh no!" Olivia said, kneeling next to the two women. She pulled down their gags and worked to remove their bonds, while Jack dragged Stuart's limp body out of the closet.

He was alive, but barely. "Frances, call 9-1-1. Muriel, tell me what happened here."

The aged woman pulled in a deep breath and rocked forward on her knees. "A man broke in through the kitchen."

"Who was he? Did you recognize him?"

"No. He was wearing a black ski mask."

Worry ground over his nerves, leaving them raw. "What did he do to Stuart?"

"I don't know. He made Stuart help him tie us up and put us in the closet." A single tear zigzagged down her plump cheek; she brushed it away. "He shoved Stuart in half an hour later. We've been in there since noon."

"Was Stuart conscious when he put him in the closet?"

"Yes."

Jack heightened his senses, listening to the thready beat of Stuart's pulse. All the terror must have caused him to have a heart attack at some point.

Frances rushed back up the stairs, out of breath. "The ambulance is on its way, sir."

"Thank you," Jack said, listening to Stuart's pulse grow weaker by the second, until it stopped completely.

"CPR, Olivia. Now!"

He ripped open the front of Stuart's shirt, sending buttons flying. "Breathe for him."

Finding his hand position, Jack started chest compressions, working in tandem with Olivia to save Stuart Redmond's life.

Chapter Thirteen

Jack put the telephone receiver back in its cradle and sat down on the edge of the bed.

The feel of Olivia's hand against his back made him close his eyes for a moment, regrouping his jumbled emotions.

"He didn't make it, Olivia."

"I'm sorry. I know you two were close."

"I need to contact Benton, but I'm not sure how to get hold of him."

"Stuart probably has an address book or something. We'll find it in the morning."

He turned to look at her, enthralled by the seductive curve of her hip draped in the sheet. At the way her hair framed her face and splayed around her on the pillow. He killed the light and slipped under the blanket.

OLIVIA GAZED AROUND the comfortable interior of the caretaker's cottage tucked in the woods between the Trayborne estate and the clinic. There was something missing, but she couldn't quite figure out what.

She moved to where Jack sat behind a large desk, sorting through paperwork, looking for contact information for Benton Redmond. So far, they'd come up empty, with the exception of learning that Stuart Redmond was penniless at the time of his death. Even she wondered where all the millions he'd inherited from Martin Trayborne had gone.

"I give up." Jack leaned back in the leather desk chair, his features pulled down in a frustrated grimace, which made her want to console him. "There's nothing here."

The grind of the front door hinges and a gust of chilly wind sliced through her sweater and brought her head around.

She half expected to see Frances or Muriel standing in the frame, but instead, a man, dressed in a black suit, stepped into the cottage and closed the door.

"Jack Trayborne?"

He stepped forward, where the light from the overhead fixture near the door illuminated his tight features. His thin lips pulled back in an almost animalistic sneer that gave her the creeps and then some. Who was he?

Tension gelled in the air, making it hard to move from the spot where she stood.

Jack came to his feet. "Benton? We've been trying to find contact information for you in your father's things. I'm sorry for your loss."

"Thanks, Jack."

"How did you learn of his death?"

"The hospital contacted me. I had work to finish up at my office in Boston before I caught the next plane out. I understand you both made a valiant effort to save him." His voice was flat and void of emotion.

"Yes, yes we did." Jack reached out and splayed his hand in the middle of her back. "You're welcome to stay as long as you need to and I'll be happy to cover the funeral expenses through the Dry Creek mortuary."

"Thank you." Benton glanced around the room before his gaze settled on her.

Repulsion skittered through her, fraying her nerve endings and erecting the tiny hairs on the back of her neck. She reached for Jack's hand behind her, unable to explain the caustic vibe emanating from the man standing in front of them. He had to be upset about his father's death. Maybe the pain of his grief was what she sensed.

"If you need anything, Benton, come up to the house."

"I will."

Jack led her out the front door, closing it behind them.

"He's a real sensitive guy." She laced her fingers in Jack's and went stride for stride with him along the narrow path back to the estate, but she found herself listening for the sound of footsteps behind them.

"Relax, Olivia. He's stoic, but he's harmless."

"How well do you know him?"

"Hardly. He was marched off to boarding school just before my parents' accident and my subsequent coma."

"He seems pretty indifferent to his father's death, but I can't be indifferent to the way he makes me feel. He gives me the creeps."

Jack squeezed her hand, resisting the urge to haul her

into the woods, lay her down in a pile of leaves and make love to her until she begged for mercy.

"How is it the hospital was able to contact him when we couldn't find one shred of information about him in his father's house? That's it, that's what was missing. Don't you find it odd there weren't any photographs of him anywhere in the cottage? Parents keep those sort of things."

She had a point, made in that beautiful, suspicious, question-asking style of hers.

"Maybe Stuart was carrying the information in his wallet, along with his son's photo. I carry an emergency contact card myself."

"Maybe, but where's his wallet?"

"Standard operating procedure. His personal effects are at the morgue with the body, waiting to be released to the mortuary and his next of kin."

"How about a drive into Black's Cove?"

Jack eyed her, his suspicions growing like a bamboo forest. She wanted to rummage in Stuart's wallet and he loved her for it, for her curiosity, grit and that insatiable need to know that motivated her into situations where she could get hurt…or worse. He sobered.

"We'll take the convertible. A top-down cruise before it's too cold."

"I'd love that." She pulled away from him, jogging down the path and around a bend just ahead of him, before disappearing into the trees beyond his line of sight.

Jack heightened his senses, feeling the need to chase

after her. The air in the woods went still, like the calm before a storm, the warning period before hell unleashed on them.

To his left, he heard a crack. The unmistakable sound of wood splintering.

Worry urged him forward. He broke into a run.

In his peripheral vision as he rounded the bend, he saw the massive tree come crashing down, taking smaller trees with it.

His heart slammed against his ribs. His palm slicked as he raised it and cast a beam of energy on the falling pine. It bobbed to a stop just above Olivia's head.

"Come to me! Hurry!"

She looked up and stepped out from under the massive bulk of limbs and needles. Certain death.

Jack scanned the woods around them, before he released the tree, letting it crash on the spot where she'd been standing a moment ago. Reaching out he took her hand and went off-trail, rounding the butt of the tree.

Its roots still held a ball of earth in their grasp. The tree had literally tipped over.

Caution hedged his bet. Natural happening or another attempt on her life? He wasn't sure.

"Come on, let's get back to the house." She clung to his arm as they worked their way around the tree stump and back out onto the trail. Death could come from anywhere, at any time; he had to stay alert.

OLIVIA FAKED INTEREST in the pictures lining the wall of the waiting area outside of the morgue.

"Please transfer Mr. Redmond's body to the Dry Creek Mortuary on 10th Street and I'll take his personal effects."

"Sign here," a young receptionist said from behind a sliding window. It looked more like a fast-food drive-through than a waiting place for the dead before they moved on to more permanent digs.

Sympathy vibrated through her and she turned around, watching the woman shove a clear plastic bag across the threshold and slide the window shut.

She all but rubbed her hands together in anticipation when she spotted the brown leather wallet in the bag along with a comb, a watch, some pocket change and Stuart's belt.

"Here," Jack said, holding the bag out to her. She took it and fell in beside him as they strode down the long corridor toward the exit.

"Whatever you can glean between now and the moment we get home, is all there is. We'll return Stuart's personal items to Benton the moment we arrive."

"For sure." Olivia glanced up, catching sight of a man pulling open the door at the end of the hallway.

Dropping back she aligned herself behind Jack.

"Jack, what are you doing here?" Benton Redmond asked, coming to a stop in front of them.

"Making arrangements for your father to be taken to the Dry Creek Mortuary."

Olivia stepped out from behind Jack and extended the bag toward him. "And picking up the effects he had on him when they took him to the hospital."

Benton's eyes narrowed for a moment before he reached out and snatched the bag from her. "You're too kind, both of you. If you'll excuse me." He turned in the direction he'd come and pushed open the door.

She let out the breath she'd been holding and stroked the wallet tucked in the pocket of her jacket. "He's such a pleasant guy. You're lucky he wasn't around when you were growing up."

Jack pressed his hand into the small of her back and steered her toward the door.

"Okay, where is it?"

"What?" she protested as he held the door open for her and she stepped outside into the afternoon sunshine.

"You know what. Is that how you conduct investigations for your stories, by lifting things that don't belong to you?" An amused smile spread on his sexy mouth and she thought her heart would pound out of her chest.

"Only when it's necessary to get at the truth. I think he's lying about the hospital calling him."

"And you're going to tell me why that matters?"

"Yes…well. I'm not sure, but someone would have had to tell him about his father's death."

The sound of squealing tires sliced into her thought process at the same instant Jack shoved her forward.

He dived for cover next to her.

A dark blue sedan lunged backward out of its parking space, just missing them.

The car shot across the parking lot with its terrified driver inside and slammed rear-end first into a light pole.

Jack came to his feet first and helped Olivia up. They sprinted across the parking lot to find the driver staggering out of his car. "What the hell happened?"

"Are you okay?" Jack asked giving him a visual once-over before pulling Olivia in next to him. Scanning the street, he spotted a silver BMW parked at the curb and watched it pull away slowly. Benton Redmond?

"Yeah, I'm fine." He rocked his head back and forth a couple of times. "I must have stepped on the gas instead of the brake. My wife's going to kill me." He walked to the rear of the car, shaking his head.

"Would you like us to call the police?"

"No. Go on, I'll be fine. The car is drivable."

Jack and Olivia turned for the car sitting in the corner of the lot.

"Wait…it's gone!"

"What's gone?" He watched her pat her jacket pockets, then pull them inside out.

"Stuart's wallet."

"Take your pick." Jack stood back, allowing Olivia to enter the massive wardrobe closet.

"They're beautiful." She stared at the costumes with her mouth open, a fact that he found amusing. It was an endearing reaction that only made him want her and need her more, but she'd yet to accept his offer to stay in Black's Cove.

Jack sobered and followed her inside. "You can be anything you want, Olivia. Cinderella to my Prince. Beauty to my Beast."

Color dished on her cheeks, her eyes becoming watery in the shallow light from overhead.

He reached for her and took her in his arms. Lowering his mouth to hers, he inhaled her scent, a sweet spicy cocktail of pheromones that sent heat racing in his veins, burning through his body, searing her to him with a fiery brand that marked her as his own, but he resisted the desire to reach for her thoughts.

"What do you know about fairy tales, Jack Trayborne?" she whispered against his lips, her voice seductively low. "This is where you sweep me off my feet and carry me away to live happily ever after."

His heart expanded in his chest as he scooped her up into his arms, headed for the bedroom down the hall. But even in his rush to have her, he couldn't shake the details of his most recent precognitive vision.

"Why so glum, Prince Charming?" She smiled and brushed her hand against the side of his cheek, sending a renewed rush of need coursing through his body. He paused at the bedroom door and stared into her eyes. "Just promise me you'll stay by my side tomorrow night at the masquerade ball. That you won't leave the house or wander away. Promise me."

A degree of fear manifested itself in Olivia's brain and stayed there as she gazed up into Jack's face. His eyes were dark blue and focused on her. His jaw set in a hard line that didn't soften. What was he hiding? What did he know that she didn't?

"What is it, Jack? What aren't you telling me?"

He entered the room and pushed the door shut with

his foot. Striding across the floor, he deposited her on the bed and lowered himself next to her.

"How long can you hold your breath?"

"A minute, maybe."

"I have a couple of requests. One, you wear a hoop slip under your gown, and two…" He reached under the pillow and pulled out a slender cylinder with a fixed air regulator attached to the top. "Do you know how to use this O2 supply?"

"No."

"Let me show you." He popped the regulator off the top. The small black mouthpiece was attached to a two-foot-long, slender hose. He clasped it in his hand. "It works like a snorkel. This goes in your mouth. Seal your lips around it and turn on the valve." He pointed out a small red knob on the top of the cylinder. "Breathe through your mouth and hold your nose. The air bubbles from your expiration will release on their own through a one-way valve. Strap it to your thigh under your dress. It carries a fifteen minute supply of oxygen. It's life, Olivia."

"That's nuts!" She tried a chuckle to go with her summation, but it lodged in her throat. She stared at Jack. He was utterly serious, and she trusted him.

"You'll know when to use it, but I pray you don't have to." His voice broke. "I'll do my best to prevent it."

"Okay, okay, I'll do what you ask." Reaching out, she cupped his cheek in her palm.

He turned and kissed it, before gazing at her again, his face placid and void of emotion.

Her heart thumped in her eardrums, blocking out everything around her but him, and she instinctively knew this was the moment. This was the instant her life would change for the better.

"I need your answer, Olivia. Will you stay in Black's Cove?"

Her throat closed as she weighed the consequences of saying no, but she knew in her heart she couldn't live without him.

"Would it aid in your decision if I told you I love you, Olivia Morgan?"

Her emotions took off for the moon. She leaned into Jack, kissing him so hard her lips hurt. "Yes. Yes, I'll stay. I love you, too, Jack." She kissed him again, drawing out the sweet sensation until she thought she'd pop.

"I could even get into the Phantom of Black's Cove thing. Maybe I can help or drive the getaway car."

She leaned into him, letting his declaration of love penetrate the layers she'd erected around her heart. Her days as a resentful vagabond were over, but a thin veil of worry covered her happiness as she squeezed the air canister in one hand and touched the man she loved with the other.

OLIVIA PARTED THE filmy curtains and stared out into the night, unsure what had woken her up. A full moon hung in the clear sky overhead and bathed everything outside the window in white light.

Their attacker was out there somewhere in the shadows, she was sure of it. Was he watching? Biding his time?

Waiting to steal the true happiness she felt for the first time in her life? A chill blanketed her skin. She shook it off, but frustration immediately replaced it.

He was strong…. Stronger than Jack?

She heard a whisper of movement in the room behind her and anticipated Jack's fingers on her skin. Soothing her doubts with his touch. Grounding her fears with his love.

A hand slammed over her mouth, driving her lip into her teeth. Blood leeched into her mouth.

Vise-like arms locked around her, knifing terror into her heart.

She struggled in the darkness, fighting against the unknown man pulling her silently toward the door.

"Jack," she screamed in silence, praying she could somehow will her voice into his head.

He dragged her out into the hallway.

"Don't fight me," he whispered, his breath hot against her ear. "He can't save you. Loving you makes him weak."

He lifted her feet off the floor and carried her down the stairs into the foyer. "I'm going to enjoy killing him and taking what is mine."

Terror flooded her heart, making her lightheaded as the madman readjusted his stance and put his arm over her throat in a choke hold.

He squeezed, cutting off her oxygen.

Olivia fought to drag another breath into her lung, but she lost the battle.

He was too strong.

"OLIVIA, WAKE UP," Jack coaxed, patting her cheek. He could hear the steady beat of her heart, hear the strong intake of her breathing. But every muscle in his body was tense as he held her in his arms where she lay in the foyer next to the open front door.

Only the single set of tracks in the frost on the cobblestones forewarned him they'd had an unwelcome visitor in the house.

She responded to his touch and opened her eyes.

"How did you get here?" he asked, helping her to sit up.

She reached for her throat and his gaze settled on the red splotch over her windpipe.

"He was here. He choked me." Her eyes narrowed and she came to her feet. He followed her up and closed the door.

Caution intertwined with the anger knotting inside of him. He'd slept through the whole damn thing. The bastard had come right into the bedroom and taken her. A show of his strength and superiority, a test of his cunning. It would be his last.

"I have to leave, Jack. I have to leave now before…"

Her words cut through the anguish cranking his emotions to the breaking point.

He reached for her thoughts, hearing the thug's words reverberating in her mind. *"I'm going to kill him and enjoy taking what is mine."*

Pulling her against him, he felt her body quake. "No. No, he won't." He held her back. A tear escaped and rolled down her cheek, then another.

"Do you love me, Olivia?"

She swallowed. "Yes."

"Then trust me. We're going to beat him." He pulled her back into his arms, fighting the flare of rage that threatened to consume him. He'd always feared its power; now he welcomed it. It was time to stand and fight.

Chapter Fourteen

Olivia eyed the influx of costume-clad guests flowing into the ballroom, trying to alleviate her anxiety. She prayed she'd made the right decision to stay. If anything happened to Jack tonight, she didn't think she could live with herself.

"You look lovely this evening." She turned at the sound of Jack's voice, staring at him in his Phantom of the Opera costume.

"So one night a year you reveal your true persona?"

"Something like that." A wicked-sexy smile parted his lips and she almost planted a kiss on them, sure the small-town rumor mill was already churning out stories of the cagey millionaire and the nosy journalist keeping him up at night.

"We can squelch those rumors, you know."

"Hey, get out of my head. I'm entitled to my thoughts, but tell me exactly how we do that? Is it a juicy story?"

"A ring. A walk down the aisle. A name change."

Warmth started in her toes and spread through her

entire body. She sobered as she looked into his eyes, and realized he was serious. It was a lethal combination to any girl's heart, but there was a buzz-kill hanging in the air and she couldn't beat it back.

"I'll think about it." She turned toward the center of the ballroom and waved him over with her finger.

The man who had so brazenly taken her from Jack's room and threatened his life could be in this room right now, hiding behind a mask, watching their every move unchallenged.

Jack took her in his arms, moving her to the smoky beat coming from the band playing in the corner. Once, twice, he brushed against her, feeling the hard form of the air supply secured beneath her gown. It was the only item not included in his precognitive vision.

Staring at the partygoers, he grasped trails of thought as he assessed each one of them. The members of a security detail he'd put in place blended easily into the swarm of guests, but he couldn't shake the suffocating cloak of foreboding that covered his nerves and played hell on his emotions.

If only he could pick the bastard out and take care of it before all hell broke loose…

The song came to an end and the event spokesman, Kyle Douglas, stepped up onto the bandstand, dressed like one of the three musketeers.

Jack heightened his senses.

"On behalf of the Trayborne Foundation, I'd like to thank our benefactor, Jack Trayborne, for once again opening his home to everyone."

A boisterous round of applause went up in the room, echoing against the high ceiling in a deafening roar that raked across his eardrums.

"If we can get you up here, Jack, I'll give you the total we raked in tonight and have you say a few words." Another rumble of applause broke out.

"Go, Jack," Olivia said from next to him, nudging him forward. "They love you and so do I."

Glancing at her, he turned his attention to the stage. Every muscle in his body refused to move, but he stepped forward, aiming for the bandstand. He could see into the future, but he couldn't prevent it from occurring; he could only intervene slightly before or after the fact.

He took the steps up onto the platform, like a man marching to the gallows.

Timing was everything.

Kyle handed him the microphone, along with a card showing the amount of money the fund-raiser had brought in. He raised the mic to his mouth, scanning the crowd, catching sight of Olivia as she slipped out of the room. Mentally, he reached out, grasping the trail of her thoughts.

Go to the water.

"We broke a record this year in fund-raising. As of this evening, ten million dollars has come into the Foundation's coffers. That's money for research that will one day save thousands of lives."

Applause rumbled through the crowd.

"Thank you and enjoy the rest of your evening. We'll see you next year." Jack handed Kyle the microphone with an ease he didn't feel.

Working his way down the steps, he was surrounded by happy guests, congratulating him and reaching out to shake his hand, but he pressed his way through the mass and lunged into the foyer outside the ballroom.

On his left, he heard the French doors leading out onto the terrace click shut.

Bolting for the exit, he pulled it open and stepped outside, spotting Olivia in her hypnotic march toward the lake a hundred yards away.

He clamped his teeth together. Restraint. He had to hang on.

She reached the dock and stepped onto it, beginning her walk to the end, past the fireworks display waiting to be launched. She paused at the edge, her form highlighted in moonlight.

Rage coursed in his veins as he took the steps down off the terrace and strode across the lawn toward her.

To his left, a man stepped out of the shadows and raised his hand, sending Olivia off the dock and into the water.

The splash sent him over the edge, but he hung on for two seconds before he rushed the madman and ran smack into a barrier he couldn't penetrate.

Olivia jolted out of her trance the instant she hit the icy water, grabbing a breath as she was yanked beneath the surface.

Down…down…down.

Struggling against an unseen force, she flailed wildly, attempting to pull herself to the top, but her feet tangled in the wet gown.

She stared at the moon above her; its watery image

appeared only inches away. Her lungs screamed for air, a trail of oxygen bubbles escaping from between her lips as she fought a losing battle.

He was too strong…

"Give it up, Jack." Benton Redmond pulled off his mask. "There's only one thing I want. The NPQ formula from your vault."

Jack lunged against the barrier again, drawing a snort from Benton.

Ten seconds.

"She's begging for air right now. Her lungs are burning. In sixty seconds she'll lose consciousness. Her sympathetic nervous system will take over and force her to breathe in the water. Six minutes, Jack, that's all the time you'll have before she's brain dead. I tried to kill her more than a couple of times, but I realized you loved her. I used her, Jack."

"You bastard." He lunged again, hitting the invisible shield protecting Benton.

Twenty seconds.

"Give it up. You can't touch me. I'm more powerful than you are."

"How, Benton, how in the hell did you get that power?"

"You should be calling me Uncle Benton. Martin Trayborne was my father."

Surprise laced through Jack, but he couldn't let it alter his plan. "You're a liar!"

Thirty seconds.

"That's what love gets you. Love makes you weak.

My father, Martin, fell in love with his lab assistant, Mildred. I'm the product of that affair, but when she saw the benefits of NPQ, she took some poor kid's dose and gave it to me instead. I eliminated all the others. I want what is rightfully mine and you're going to give it to me or she dies."

Forty seconds.

"And what about Stuart? You siphoned off all of his money."

"Stupid old man. He never figured it out and when I told him, he had a damn heart attack."

"You bastard." Jack circled him, feeling rage fire in his body. Energy surged through him in hot jolts he fought to control.

Fifty seconds.

Benton reached out and dragged Olivia to the surface of the water. "I want it, Jack! I want the formula now! Open that damn impenetrable vault or I'll drown her."

Jack heard Olivia gasp for air, saw the silhouette of her head just above the water.

Now, Olivia.

Benton shoved her under again.

Letting out a guttural yell, he lunged for Benton, raising his energy shield.

The two opposing fields smashed into one another and short-circuited in a zap of heat and sparks that lit up the night.

Jack went airborne, hitting the ground with a thud that forced the air out of his lungs.

Benton recovered first, tearing the overhead power

line from its service box on the side of the cottage and thrusting it at him.

Jumping to his feet, Jack lunged right. The wire hissed past, just missing his face, and shot up into the air like a whip.

Reaching out, Jack cast an energy field around Benton, trapping him before he could regroup for another strike.

"No!" Benton staggered forward.

The live wire lashed out, snapping like a wet towel, as it flicked the shield around Benton, before rearing back and becoming entangled in a tree high overhead.

An arc shot toward Jack. He aborted the field and fell back, avoiding the aura of electricity spider-webbing around Benton.

Benton's eyes went wide.

The electricity penetrated the barrier by degrees until it breached the shell and zapped into Benton's body.

He took the two-hundred-amp charge, convulsing like a fish on land until he collapsed on the ground in a smoldering heap.

Horrified, Jack came to his feet and rushed forward. Heightening his senses, he searched for a pulse.

Nothing, There was nothing he could do for Benton Redmond. His heart had stopped.

Jack turned and sprinted for the lake, looking for Olivia to surface as he ran the length of the dock and stared down into the water.

Spotting movement just under the surface, he reached for her, encircled her and dragged her toward him from the depths.

Raising her from the water, he deposited her on the end of the dock, where she went to her knees and pulled the air regulator out of her mouth.

"Damn, I'm sorry I had to do that." He knelt next to her and took her in his arms.

"Is he dead?" She nodded toward the spot where Benton lay sprawled on the lawn.

"Yes."

"How…how did you kill him?"

"I didn't. He tried to electrocute me, but it got him instead. His vulnerability was holding you underwater, leaving him a single ability to fight me."

"How did you know I'd need this?" She dropped the air canister on the dock with a thud and he pushed it off into the lake.

"I've got secrets you've yet to uncover. The only thing you need to know is love makes you strong. Love invokes trust. You trusted what I asked you to do. You saved yourself."

Olivia let her head lull against Jack's chest, feeling the first violent shiver rip through her body. She was the coldest she'd ever been on the outside, but on the inside, a steady stream of heat spread through her.

"Someday you'll stop talking to me in riddles, Jack Trayborne."

"Never." Jack lifted her up into his arms and strode up the dock. "Come on. Let's get you inside and dry. The authorities will be here soon with a barrage of questions."

"I'm going to write a feature story about this, you know."

"About my soon-to-be wife falling into the lake, being sucked down by her wet gown? About the tragic accident that took the life of a guest as he raced to save her. By the way, there's a job opening at the *Gazette*. They'll be calling you Monday morning."

She reached for his chin, pulled his face in line with hers and kissed him.

Epilogue

Five Months Later

Olivia couldn't stop her hand from shaking as she brushed the top of Ross's head, smoothing his hair in a nervous gesture.

Five months of waiting for the formula to be produced boiled down to this one moment.

Jack pulled the plunger down on the syringe, filling the hypodermic with NPQ. This was Ross's dose, the one that had been stolen from him all those years ago by Mildred Redmond and given to her son, Benton, instead. It was only right that he received it now.

Tears burned the back of Olivia's eyes. There were so many possibilities ahead. Her and Jack's wedding was less than three months away and she'd have her baby brother back...whole again?

Jack shoved the needle into the IV line and depressed the plunger. He'd already reached for Ross's thoughts and found his mind active and filled with questions much like his sister's was most of the time.

Glancing over Ross's head, he gazed at her, witnessing the broad grin on her lips, and he found himself praying Ross's awakening would be everything she needed. The annihilation of her guilt and resentment.

The clinic had been razed. It was a new beginning for them all.

Ross's fingers started to twitch, uncoordinated movements that slowly fell into sync.

Excitement pulsed in Jack's body. He knelt next to Ross, searching his face for signs of cognitive thought.

A weak noise rumbled in his throat, rising out in a burst of sound.

Jack felt Olivia's hand on his shoulder. He reached up to cover it.

It was working. The NPQ was working. Putting Ross's broken pathways back together, stimulating his motor skills.

Granted, there were months of physical therapy ahead, but they had therapists lined up and ready to help.

"Liv… Liv…." The name formed and sputtered from his mouth.

Olivia couldn't believe it. She knelt in front of her brother. "I'm here, Ross. I'm right here." Reaching up, she pressed her hand to his cheek, staring into his eyes and seeing recognition for the first time in thirty years.

He was going to make it. He was going to come back to her.

A smile tugged on one side of Ross's mouth and her heart squeezed. She had Jack to thank for this miracle.

It was true. Love made you strong. And she planned to be the strongest woman in the world.

* * * * *

Celebrate 60 years of
pure reading pleasure with Harlequin®!

Harlequin Presents® is proud to introduce its
gripping new miniseries,
THE ROYAL HOUSE OF KAREDES.
An exquisite coronation diamond,
split as a symbol of a warring royal family's feud,
is missing! But whoever reunites the diamond
halves will rule all....

Welcome to eight brand-new titles that unfold
to reveal the stories of kings and queens, princes
and princesses torn apart by pride and power,
but finally reunited by love.

Step into the world of Karedes with
BILLIONAIRE PRINCE, PREGNANT MISTRESS
Available July 2009
from Harlequin Presents®.

ALEXANDROS KAREDES, SNOW DUSTING the shoulders of his leather jacket and glittering like jewels in his dark hair, stood at the door. Maria felt the blood drain from her head.

"Good evening, Ms. Santos."

His voice was as she remembered it. Deep. Husky. Perfect English, but with the faintest hint of a Greek accent. And cold, as cold as it had been that awful morning she would never forget, when he'd accused her of horrible things, called her terrible names....

"Aren't you going to ask me in?"

She fought for composure. Last time they'd faced each other, they'd been on his turf. Now they were on hers. She was in command here, and that meant everything.

"There's a sign on the door downstairs," she said, her tone every bit as frigid as his. "It says, 'No soliciting or vagrants.'"

His lips drew back in a wolfish grin. "Very amusing."

"What do you want, Prince Alexandros?"

A tight smile eased across his mouth and it killed her

that even now, knowing he was a vicious, arrogant man, she couldn't help but notice what a handsome mouth it was. Chiseled. Generous. Beautiful, like the rest of him, which made him living proof that beauty could, indeed, be only skin deep.

"Such formality, Maria. You were hardly so proper the last time we were together."

She knew his choice of words was deliberate. She felt her face heat; she couldn't help that but she damned well didn't have to let him lure her into a verbal sparring match.

"I'll ask you once more, your highness. What do you want?"

"Ask me in and I'll tell you."

"I have no intention of asking you in. Tell me why you're here or don't. It's your choice, just as it will be my choice to shut the door in your face."

He laughed. It infuriated her but she could hardly blame him. He was tall—six two, six three—and though he stood with one shoulder leaning against the door frame, hands tucked casually into the pockets of the jacket, his pose was deceptive. He was strong, with the leanly muscled body of a well-trained athlete.

She remembered his body with painful clarity. The feel of him under her hands. The power of him moving over her. The taste of him on her tongue.

Suddenly, he straightened, his laughter gone. "I have not come this distance to stand in your doorway," he said coldly, "and I am not going to leave until I am ready to do so. I suggest you stand aside and stop behaving like a petulant child."

A petulant child? Was that what he thought? This man who had spent hours making love to her and had then accused her of—of trading her body for profit?

Except it had not been love, it had been sex. And the sooner she got rid of him, the better.

She let go of the doorknob and stepped aside. "You have five minutes."

He strolled past her, bringing cold air and the scent of the night with him. She swung toward him, arms folded. He reached past her, pushed the door closed, then folded his arms, too. She wanted to open the door again but she'd be damned if she was going to get into a who's-in-charge-here argument with him. She was in charge, and he would surely see a tussle over the ground rules as a sign of weakness.

Instead, she looked past him at the big clock above her work table.

"Ten seconds gone," she said briskly. "You're wasting time, your highness."

"What I have to say will take longer than five minutes."

"Then you'll just have to learn to economize. More than five minutes, I'll call the police."

Instantly, his hand was wrapped around her wrist. He tugged her toward him, his dark-chocolate eyes almost black with anger.

"You do that and I'll tell every tabloid shark I can contact about how Maria Santos tried to buy a five-hundred-thousand-dollar commission by seducing a prince." He smiled thinly. "They'll lap it up."

* * * * *

What will it take for this billionaire prince to realize
he's falling in love with his mistress...?
Look for
BILLIONAIRE PRINCE, PREGNANT MISTRESS
by Sandra Marton
Available July 2009
from Harlequin Presents®.

We'll be spotlighting a different series every month throughout 2009 to celebrate our 60th anniversary.

Look for Harlequin® Presents in July!

TWO CROWNS, TWO ISLANDS, ONE LEGACY

A royal family, torn apart by pride and its lust for power, reunited by purity and passion

Step into the world of Karedes beginning this July with

BILLIONAIRE PRINCE, PREGNANT MISTRESS
by
Sandra Marton

Eight volumes to collect and treasure!

In 2009 Harlequin celebrates
60 years of pure reading pleasure!

We're marking this occasion by offering
16 **FREE** full books to download and read.

Visit

www.HarlequinCelebrates.com

to choose from a variety of
great romance stories
that are absolutely **FREE!**

(Total approximate retail value of $60)

We invite you to visit and share the Web site
with your friends, family
and anyone who enjoys reading.

From *New York Times*
bestselling authors

CARLA NEGGERS
SUSAN MALLERY
KAREN HARPER

More Than Words:
STORIES OF
STRENGTH

They're your neighbors, your aunts, your sisters and your best friends. They're women across North America committed to changing and enriching lives, one good deed at a time. Three of these exceptional women have been selected as recipients of Harlequin's More Than Words award. And three *New York Times* bestselling authors have kindly offered their creativity to write original short stories inspired by these real-life heroines.

Visit **www.HarlequinMoreThanWords.com**
to find out more, or to nominate
a real-life heroine in your life.

Proceeds from the sale of this book will be reinvested in Harlequin's charitable initiatives.

Available in March 2009 wherever books are sold.

INTRODUCING THE FIFTH ANNUAL
MORE THAN WORDS ANTHOLOGY

Five bestselling authors
Five real-life heroines

A little comfort, caring and compassion go a long way toward making the world a better place. Just ask the dedicated women handpicked from countless worthy nominees across North America to become this year's recipients of Harlequin's More Than Words award. To celebrate their accomplishments, five bestselling authors have honored the winners by writing short stories inspired by these real-life heroines.

Visit **www.HarlequinMoreThanWords.com**
to find out more, or to nominate
a real-life heroine in your life.

Proceeds from the sale of this book will be reinvested in Harlequin's charitable initiatives.

Available in April 2009 wherever books are sold.

You're invited to join our Tell Harlequin Reader Panel!

By joining our new reader panel you will:

- Receive Harlequin® books—they are FREE and yours to keep with no obligation to purchase anything!
- Participate in fun online surveys
- Exchange opinions and ideas with women just like you
- Have a say in our new book ideas and help us publish the best in women's fiction

In addition, you will have a chance to win great prizes and receive special gifts!
See Web site for details. Some conditions apply.
Space is limited.

To join, visit us at
www.TellHarlequin.com.

REQUEST YOUR FREE BOOKS!

2 FREE NOVELS PLUS 2 FREE GIFTS!

HARLEQUIN®

INTRIGUE®

Breathtaking Romantic Suspense

YES! Please send me 2 FREE Harlequin Intrigue® novels and my 2 FREE gifts (gifts are worth about $10). After receiving them, if I don't wish to receive any more books, I can return the shipping statement marked "cancel." If I don't cancel, I will receive 6 brand-new novels every month and be billed just $4.24 per book in the U.S. or $4.99 per book in Canada. That's a savings of close to 15% off the cover price! It's quite a bargain! Shipping and handling is just 50¢ per book.* I understand that accepting the 2 free books and gifts places me under no obligation to buy anything. I can always return a shipment and cancel at any time. Even if I never buy another book from Harlequin, the two free books and gifts are mine to keep forever.

182 HDN EYTR 382 HDN EYT3

Name _____ (PLEASE PRINT)

Address _____ Apt. #

City _____ State/Prov. _____ Zip/Postal Code

Signature (if under 18, a parent or guardian must sign)

Mail to the **Harlequin Reader Service:**
IN U.S.A.: P.O. Box 1867, Buffalo, NY 14240-1867
IN CANADA: P.O. Box 609, Fort Erie, Ontario L2A 5X3

Not valid to current subscribers of Harlequin Intrigue books.

**Are you a current subscriber of Harlequin Intrigue books
and want to receive the larger-print edition?
Call 1-800-873-8635 today!**

* Terms and prices subject to change without notice. Prices do not include applicable taxes. Sales tax applicable in N.Y. Canadian residents will be charged applicable provincial taxes and GST. Offer not valid in Quebec. This offer is limited to one order per household. All orders subject to approval. Credit or debit balances in a customer's account(s) may be offset by any other outstanding balance owed by or to the customer. Please allow 4 to 6 weeks for delivery. Offer available while quantities last.

Your Privacy: Harlequin is committed to protecting your privacy. Our Privacy Policy is available online at www.eHarlequin.com or upon request from the Reader Service. From time to time we make our lists of customers available to reputable third parties who may have a product or service of interest to you. If you would prefer we not share your name and address, please check here. ☐

HI09R

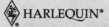

HARLEQUIN®

INTRIGUE®

COMING NEXT MONTH

Available July 14, 2009

#1143 SHOWDOWN IN WEST TEXAS by Amanda Stevens
Her photo is in the hands of a hit man, but she has no idea. Lucky for her, an ex-cop stumbled upon the would-be killer...and he's determined to protect the woman whose face he can't forget.

#1144 SHE'S POSITIVE by Dolores Fossen
Kenner County Crime Unit
After discovering she's pregnant, the hotshot FBI agent's soon-to-be ex-wife falls into the hands of a dangerous criminal. He'll do anything to save her life and their second chance at love.

#1145 SMALL-TOWN SECRETS by Debra Webb
Colby Agency: Elite Reconnaissance Division
Only a top investigator at the Colby Agency can help her confront the dark secrets of her childhood—and give her the love and protection she needs for the future they desire together.

#1146 PREGNESIA by Carla Cassidy
The Recovery Men
While working at Recovery Inc., a former navy SEAL repossesses a car...which just happens to have an unconscious pregnant woman in the backseat. Unwilling to let her and her unborn child come to harm, he's ready to shield her for the long-term.

#1147 MOUNTAIN INVESTIGATION by Jessica Andersen
Bear Claw Creek Crime Lab
She was just a means to an end—use her to find the murderers of his colleagues. But the sexy target rouses more than just the FBI agent's need for revenge as they brave the wilds of Colorado in search of an elusive killer....

#1148 CAPTIVE OF THE DESERT KING by Donna Young
A king finds himself attracted to an assertive American reporter, but past hurts have made him suspicious of women. When rebels shoot down their plane, they are in a race across the desert for their lives... and love.

www.eHarlequin.com

HICNMBPA0609